I0547492

Also available from Leone Sperling

Coins for the Ferryman

Oasis

What About Love?

Jamie

Book of Life

Two powerful and controversial novellas comprise this ironically-titled book, in which very bizarre mother- child relationships are explored.

The characters in MOTHER'S DAY all believe that perfection is possible, that destiny can be controlled, that disorder can be kept at bay, and that actions occur without consequences.

MOTHER'S DAY is disturbing and disconcerting; its uncluttered and direct style adds to its rawness. The writing is individual and makes for gripping reading. It makes us examine our lives to see how far we manage to keep disorder at bay by ignoring it. And it makes us wonder how narrowly we have escaped fates similar to theirs.

This is LEONE SPERLING'S second book, originally published in 1984 by Wild & Woolley, Produced by Redress Press.

Her first book, COINS FOR THE FERRYMAN was published by Pan Books (Australia) in 1981 and is now available in a new edition through Cilento Publishing.

MOTHER'S DAY

A novel by Leone Sperling

© Leone Sperling 1984, 2014

Leone Sperling asserts the moral right to be identified as the author of 'Mother's Day'.

Cover design and typeset by Green Avenue Design.

Cover illustration by Angelique King.

First Published in 1984 by Wild and Woolley Pty Limited.

This edition published by Cilento Publishing, Sydney Australia.

ISBN: 978-0-9925601-7-1

All rights reserved. No part of this publication may be reproduced, stored in a retrieval system, or transmitted, in any form or by any means, electronic, mechanical, photocopying, recording or otherwise, without the prior permission of the publishers.

For Janet Blake Neild, who taught me that I could turn chaos into creativity.

THANATOS

HATE

This is the story of a mother and daughter who hated each other with great passion. They would, if they could, have carved each other up into pieces and thrown the pieces into garbage bags and hurled the garbage bags into the sea. And they would, if possible, have sawed up each other's bones to make sure that there was no chance of resurrection.

They were not aware of their hatred for each other. They would have been surprised to learn that, beneath the flooding warmth of love, there grew an ugly thing of such diabolic power that it needed only the touch of one man to bring it to monstrous life.

A man entered their lives and fed their fire and touched off their tragedy until it had no choice but to hurl itself to its determined end.

EVE

Tragedy makes no sense if you look at it in isolation. Murder is meaningless unless you see it as the ultimate act of self immolation and so it is necessary to look at Eve – slim-hipped, narrow-pelvised. Skinny, you would call her if you saw her gliding down the street. Long, frizzy, mousy hair she has and her top teeth protrude. Her narrow lips cannot cover this projection and, in repose, her upper teeth rest on her lower lip. And the protrusion of the teeth is uneven so that the curve is more obvious on the right hand side of her face. It is not unattractive and rest of her face is lean and smooth and white. She has light brown eyes and a long, thin neck. Her hands are slender and delicate. Her breasts are small and her hips don't curve and yet she carries herself, as she walks down the street, with a feminine elegance and grace. Eve.

EVE AND THE BABY

The most significant thing about Eve, a thing you would not notice immediately, is that she is carrying a baby. The baby is glued into her neck so tightly that you would be forgiven if you did not notice it at all. Once someone stopped her in the street and asked to see the baby. She had to pull the baby off her and turn it to the sun for inspection. It was a very difficult thing to do. It was difficult for Eve and it was difficult for the baby because they were inseparable and whenever there was a space between them their bodies felt as if they had been peeled raw and they were both drawn by a magnetic need to get their skins back together again. The person who asked to see the baby did not understand this. In fact the person was so insensitive as to ask Eve what the baby's name was. Quite understandably, Eve was shocked. The baby had no name. How can you give a separate name to a small area of you own skin?

THE BABY

And how did the baby feel about all of this? The baby felt just fine. It was a very lucky baby. For most of us birth means the beginning of being alone. This baby was never alone. Eve had given her baby an outside womb and the baby, naturally enough, was content to stay there. And who can blame the baby for that? Being happy, resting snug forever in its warm mother womb.

ORDER

Eve was a hermit. No doubt, once upon a time, she had a mother and a father. Perhaps she had a sister or a brother. Long ago, there must have been laughter and tears. Certainly she had known passion and despair, heartbreak and happiness, pain and joy but she had decided, for some reason, that the world of men and women was not for her. The only problem attached to such a decision was that, deep within her, she felt an aching urgency to bear a child and so she went out into the world and got pregnant as quickly as possible and, as soon as she was certain that the child was growing there, inside her womb, she locked herself away again.

She lived in a small house, with a small garden and everything in her house and in her garden was perfectly in order. Neat and flawless, tidy and clean. She could not tolerate chaos. Perhaps that is why she found the world of men and women so distasteful.

She saw that there was some kind of pattern in the universe and she attempted to take this order and distill it and extract its essence and pour it into her house and into her garden and into her womb.

Eve never allowed the slightest thing to disturb her. She maintained, at all times, a sense of harmonious equilibrium, a cool and balanced calm.

She had no telephone and if anyone dared to knock on her door she simply behaved as if they hadn't knocked at all. She had the power to annihilate anyone.

People thought she was peculiar.

ROTTEN LITTLE BASTARD

At the same time, a few hundred miles away, in the children's ward of a hospital devoted to treating sufferers of tuberculosis, a five-year-old boy was visiting his eight-year-old girlfriend. He was supposed to stay in his own bed but some inner compulsion kept drawing him to hers. He would lie in the crook of her mothering arm, his little cheek resting on her chest, his arm across her belly. Every now and then she would nuzzle into him and kiss him on the lips His stiff little prick lay exquisitely on her thigh. Sometimes she would put her hand down underneath the covers and let her pudgy fingers touch his erection. When she did this he was suffused with an indescribable feeling for which he did not have a name. Sometimes she took his left hand and placed it on her gently swelling mound and they rested like that for a long time. They could have stayed that way forever.

The nursing staff did not approve of this kind of behaviour and whenever they came across our cuddling couple, cocooned in ecstasy, the nurses would shout at them and tear them viciously apart and smack his bum and send him crying back to bed and say, 'You rotten little bastard!' No one blamed the girl.

Sometimes he would hide in the girls' toilets and wait for the girl to come in. When he heard the tinkle of her pee in the toilet, his penis would grow stiff and he would rub it – up and down, up and down, up and down. He didn't know why. He would have liked her to pee all over him.

CHAOS

Eve's problem was her belief that life could be lived totally within the constraints of harmony and peace. Her own life was ordered. She felt pure mother-love for her baby. She thought such a way of life could go on forever. She was wrong. She was wrong because she did not understand that order can be achieved only by chiselling it out of disorder; that peace is possible only if one is able to come to terms with war and that pure love can be attained only through standing face to face with hatred. She did not admit to the existence of opposites in herself, and, because the baby was part of herself, she didn't allow for the existence of opposites in the baby. Eve did not understand the principle of human paradox.

The baby, like all babies, was chaos. The baby sucked and fed; it gooed and smiled; it cuddled and snuggled. But the baby also screamed and cried and punched and hit and tore and bit. The baby was full of vomit and piss and shit. And whenever the baby tried to declare its violence, to screech its hatred or to thunder its murderous rage, Eve, although she felt afraid, made herself meet the baby with controlled and invulnerable calm.

The baby, who did not know that she was a separate being, began to see in Eve's face the mirror of her own aggression. Eve's protruding teeth became leering fangs in a cannibal face.

And so a war began between them and they lost their oneness because Eve did not know how to meet the diffusion of the baby's chaos and the baby did not know how to meet the wall of Eve's pervading order.

The baby's belly echoed with hunger but when the warm milk hit its emptiness, the baby's stomach contracted into a sharp fist and flung the poison back up to the surface again and hot milk and bile spurted out onto Eve's neat cleanliness.

Eve's breast seemed to swell into a giant, pulsating, suffocating mound of flesh and the baby had to arch away in order to keep breathing. Eve was terrified of the baby and the baby was terrified of Eve.

Eve decided that she had lost the battle and she gave the baby a bottle to drink from. When the baby came to understand the neutrality of the bottle, it decided that it might as well stay alive after all.

At this stage, Eve gave the baby a name. She called the baby Ruth because she remembered the stories from the Bible and she hoped that this daughter would dwell in harmony with her mother forever.

From that time on, both Eve and the baby tried hard to ignore the existence of chaos.

STATE OF TRUCE

And so, a state of truce was declared between Eve and her baby, Ruth. The baby would have liked to shit all over her mother but instead she wiped her faeces on the wall above her cot. At meal times, when she had eaten enough, she would tip her unfinished food over her head while Eve wasn't looking. At odd times she was overwhelmed by an impulse to pee on the potplants.

Apart from these few small lapses, the baby found it safer to live in Eve's image rather than in her own. The baby had learned a very good lesson. She had learned that aggression could easily lead to death. So she gave up murder and settled for conformity.

As Ruth grew from a baby into a little girl, she developed a pliable and obliging disposition, an exotic and unusual delicacy, a dark and sensuous beauty. When Eve and Ruth walked down the street, passers-by would respond to the child with spontaneous admiration. Although Eve maintained her hermit-like existence, she could not help feeling pride in her child's ability to captivate the attention of those about her.

Eve did not seek the outside world but Ruth was hungry for it and she brought to her mother's house bits and pieces of external reality – a leaf, a flower, a stray cat, a playmate. And so, whether Eve liked it or not, her daughter's vitality gently led her back into a wider world.

There was just one strange and disturbing thing about the child. No matter how many people told Ruth that she was beautiful, she persisted in believing that she was ugly. Perhaps she sensed an unseen ugliness that grew inside her.

THE DIRTY ROTTEN LITTLE BASTARD

Meanwhile, the little boy with the stiff prick, had been growing up and it is necessary, before proceeding any further, to tell you two stories about him.

When he was eleven years old, the little boy, whose name was Jonathan, discovered how pleasant it was to masturbate and, quite understandably, brought himself to joyful orgasm as every available opportunity. His mother did not approve of such activities. One night she got up to go to the toilet and she heard him masturbating. She went into his room and screamed at him: 'Stop playing with yourself, you dirty rotten little bastard!'

She hit him and hit him and hit him. She was wearing a nylon nightie and her big triangle of hair was clearly visible. The more she hit him, the more her big breasts wobbled and the closer view he got of her wide, hairy cunt. The more she hit him the more excited he became. She grabbed his wrist and tried to take his hand away from his cock but he wouldn't let go and he laughed and laughed at her and kept hold of his cock and he pulled it harder and harder and she snatched at his hand again to pull it away but, in doing so, she touched him and her touch triggered his climax and his cock spat and spurted hot sperm all over her angry hand. Horrified, she ran to the bathroom and hastily washed off his filth and she was shaking and sobbing and she could not understand at all what she had done to deserve such a disgusting, dirty little boy.

The second story about Jonathan is one that turned him, irrevocably, from a dirty boy into a bad boy.

When Jonathan was fourteen years old he was besotted with a beautiful lady of twenty-four. She was the daughter of an old man for whom Jonathan did odd jobs. Having no father, Jonathan had developed a respect and love for the old man, at the same time as he lusted after the daughter. He longed to fuck her, but, being only fourteen years old, he had no hope of having his dream come true.

One day, when the old man and his daughter were out, Jonathan broke into their house. He knew that what he was doing was wrong but a compulsion drove him into her room. At first he did not know what it was that he had to do but he found himself opening the drawers where she kept her underclothes and he emptied them all out onto the bed. He heaped her brassieres and pants and stockings into a soft pile. Then he took off all his clothes and he lay down on the bed and he wound her stockings around him and draped her petticoats on his thighs and pulled her pants over his face and he cupped her brassiere in his hands and he lay on the bed and pretended that her long, black hair was falling over his face and he felt the warmth of her breasts press against his narrow chest and his cock rose to meet her cunt and she rode him frantically to his climax and he exploded in her underclothes and then he lay there, quite content.

He stayed in her room for a long while and he made himself climax again and again and he wanked all over her pillow and in her sheets and on her bedspread and then he got up and he got dressed and he left the house.

The old man and his daughter realized who had made this disgusting mess and the police came. He appeared before a magistrate who sent him to a reform school.

And now you know all that is relevant for the part Jonathan is to play in the lives of Eve and her daughter, Ruth.

EVE'S DREAMS

Eve awakes with her mouth full of dreams and a fabric of symbols sliding across her skin but she swallows some of the images down and flicks the others away and if you were to ask her what she has been dreaming about she would reply that she has not dreamed at all. She would say that she has slept profoundly, untroubled and untouched by outward or inward cares. If you pursued the matter any further, she would state, quite firmly, that she never dreams at all. She has no need of dreams. Her dream is the reality of her fifteen-year-old daughter, lying asleep in the next room, sprawled in soft purple.

Summer is whispering to Eve but Eve, who is now forty, stopped listening long ago. She has allowed herself to rust, to rot, to turn to mould and the green tendrils of her being never see the sun.

She is content to remain where she is. The venetian blinds are closed. She is encircled by soft cotton curtains; enclosed by ivory walls; wrapped in neat, white sheets. She is satisfied. She has rid herself of momentary darkness. She has cleansed herself of dreams.

RUTH'S DREAMS

Ruth dreams wild – of mountains and rivers and jungles and seas. She soars through the skies, spirals past the planets, spins beyond the sun, turns and tumbles, plunges to the ocean, slices through the waves, thunders up the hill tops, hovers and glides in the warm still air, slides naked in the stream of her dreams.

She is wide when she awakes – spread-eagled, spacious, broad across the bed. She moves a hand to try to close her open space but still it gapes – a wide-eyed, weeping, yawning slit. She is hollowed helpless. Her hand rests moist on her secret self and then she lifts her fingers to touch her mouth. Slowly, she paints her lips with her own wetness and then allows her tongue to make a leisurely journey across her mouth to taste and take in the bitterness of her being. The tang of her essence stabs into her nostrils and she breathes in, hard and deep, the satisfaction of her own smell.

Suddenly she can relax and move and now she is able to bridge the gap between her thighs. She snuggles and curls in her soft, flower-patterned sheets and notices, with pleasure, how the mauves and purples echo in her bedclothes and her wall-paper and her curtains.

Summer is calling to Ruth and Ruth hears the urgency of its cries. She bounds from her bed and rushes to the bathroom. She puts the plug in the bath tub and turns the taps on full. She wants to join the day. While she is waiting for the bath to fill she looks at her face in the mirror. Tenderly she kisses her imaged self. The glass is cool and dry.

THE BATH

A golden hue hugs the corners of the bathroom; brown and yellow tiles hum in the sun and send sparkling smiles to each other. The streaks of light and the swirls of steam meet and mingle and Ruth stands at the moist centre of their coalescence and sinks her toes deep into the thick bath mat. She stands for a moment, lost in the misty warmth. Then she turns off the water taps and hops into the bath.

She hears a click. The door of the bathroom opens. She does not turn her head but she can feel Eve's presence in the room. Eve goes to the handbasin opposite the bath. She runs the cold water and splashes her face. She reaches for a towel and dries herself. She takes down her toothbrush and carefully squeezes the toothpaste onto it. She does not look at Ruth.

As she brushes her teeth she lets her eyes look into the mirror. You might think she is watching herself clean her teeth but she is not. She is allowing herself to use this pretence so that she can look at Ruth's reflection in the mirror. Her hand trembles as her eyes rest on her daughter's body and she scrubs her teeth all the more vigorously to hide the trembling, not only from her child but from herself.

She rinses her mouth out with cold water and spits the water into the basin. She picks up the towel and wipes her face dry. She looks at herself in the mirror. She examines her teeth. She runs her tongue across them. She looks as if she is totally absorbed in making sure that she has cleaned her teeth properly. What she is really doing is mentally preparing herself for the thing she is about to say. She picks up a brush and begins to do her hair. She brushes carefully, meticulously and all the time that she seems to be absorbed in brushing her hair she is really gathering herself together, fortifying herself, assembling the necessary courage to be able to say the thing she is about to say.

Then she turns to Ruth and smiles. 'Let me wash you,' says Eve. She tries to hide the eagerness that rises in her throat. Ruth looks at Eve. She surveys her mother. She deliberately takes her time to answer. Eve can feel her daughter's eyes scanning her and she makes a great effort to squash herself down, to keep herself calm. She refuses to allow her hungry fingertips to move and betray her longing. She waits.

Ruth smiles. 'Alright,' she says. Eve lets go. She can feel herself filling up with relief and desire.

And so the ritual begins.

Eve bends down beside the bath. She takes the washer and wets it in the warm bath water. With one hand she washes the girl's face, slowly and lovingly, while the other hand holds the young face firm, touching it from soft, curved cheek to rounded chin. Ruth closes her eyes and submits herself to the caressing mother hands.

Eve takes her time. She puts soap on the washer and washes each hand in turn, rubbing deep down between the hollows of the fingers, circling the palm, working her way slowly to the tip of each finger. Next she washes each arm, starting at the wrist and moving upwards to the shoulder, curving in to clean the shadowy crevices of her daughter's neck.

Ruth keeps her eyes closed but this scene has been enacted so many times before that she understands exactly the part she is to play. She knows intuitively when to lift first her right arm and then her left so that Eve exposes and washes the dark furrows of her armpits. As she washes Ruth's under-arms, Eve manages to brush the gentle curve of her daughter's breasts.

Ruth sits up quickly and opens her eyes. Eve hastily stands and, in a businesslike way, vigorously scrubs the girl's back. Ruth then lets herself slide back into the water and allows her eyes to close again.

This is the signal for the beginning of the moment that each of them both fears and longs for. Eve rinses the soap out of the washer and squeezes the water out of it and then folds it neatly and puts it on the side of the bath. She kneels down again beside the bath and reaches for the soap. As she carefully soaps her hands she can feel the familiar dryness in her mouth and the quivering in the centre of her being. Gently, sensuously, she massages each breast, letting her fingers trace a path to the sweet, pink nipples, feeling them harden beneath her touch. The moment has about it the precious quality of timelessness. The very finest line exists between the exquisite and the unbearable and, at just the right moment, Eve lets her hands move on to wash the flat belly and then, with the excitement of the breasts still hanging between them, she allows a momentary, lingering touch of the clitoris before travelling swiftly on to the energetic task of scrubbing thighs and knees and calves and feet. As Eve washes the soles of Ruth's feet, Ruth laughs and breaks the spell. She jumps up from the bath and reaches for a towel.

'Let me dry you,' whispers Eve.

'No,' laughs Ruth and wraps her secret self into the big, golden towel and Eve tries to push aside her disappointment while she bends down and pulls out the plug and lets the water run out of the bath.

Eve stands up straight and then begins, quite busily, to tidy up the bathroom. She hopes that Ruth will ignore her presence and start to dry herself. But Ruth knows exactly what her mother wants from her and an essential, if obstinate, part of herself has decided, on this particular occasion, not to give her mother the thing she is asking for. So Ruth stays as she is. She holds the towel firmly around herself and waits. Eve soon runs out of things to do in the bathroom so she has to give in and leave the room. She leaves the door open but Ruth deliberately closes it and locks it. When she is quite alone, Ruth lets the towel drop onto the floor and examines her own nakedness.

JONATHAN'S DREAMS

Twenty-year-old Jonathan dreams. His dreams stain and smear, slurring filth through his mind, soiling the foul corners of the locked rooms that haunt his nightly voyages. The coarse walls close in about him, stifling, suffocating, and, in the despair of his dreams, his body opens up and weeps and pisses and shits and his hand fumbles through the floor of his own foulness to find the key and he slides and sinks in a sea of shit. He cries for help and stretches out his hand in the hope that his gaoler might hear him and pity him and save him once again. He feels the shit rising around him. It has almost reached his throat. He is sure that he will choke. The taste of excrement fills his mouth. And then, deep in his dreams, someone opens the door and his filth floods away and he is left panting and helpless and naked and wailing.

She comes into the room, her hugeness filling the space around him, replacing the foul air with a cunt-sweet mother smell. He longs to be cradled and bathed and cuddled and fed. And she, the giant gaoler of his sleeping self, bundles him up in her vast arms and her big, white breasts balloon above him and he nuzzles home and his little tongue searches and finds the rubbery, pink nipple and his lips close around it and he sucks and drinks and gulps and swallows until his belly is full of her love.

And then she lays him gently in the centre of a downy bed and with her big red tongue she licks him clean. She licks his back and his bottom, his legs and his arms, the folds of his neck. She teases him with her tongue. She nibbles and eats and licks his prick until it stands erect. She takes its tip into her mouth and puts her tongue in the slit. She works her tongue round and round its straining head. She slides her mouth up and down its quivering length. Then she sucks the throbbing tip back into her mouth. He opens his eyes. He wants to see her face. But when he looks he sees, with horror, that she is not a woman. A large, dark, furry animal is eating his prick; its thick lips hang red and wet; its eager tongue wide and hot. He tries to push it away and his hands take hold of its woolly head but the animal cannot leave his prick alone. It longs for, it needs, it is obsessed with his prick. The animal nudges and snuffles and snorts and demands his prick again and takes it hungrily into its lusty mouth. Jonathan is helpless. He cannot fight against such passion and so he lies back and submits to the animal and allows his own desire to well and ebb and rise and flood and he wakes to find his penis pumping hot over his sweating skin and he fills the bed with his own wet warmth.

RUB ME

Jonathan jumps up out of his sticky, boarding-house bed and goes to the bathroom. He stands under the shower and scrubs himself clean of dreams and as the water flows over his lean body he decides that what he needs to do, on this sunny Sunday, is to go hunting for someone to fuck. So he washes his hair and vigorously massages his scalp. He carefully rinses away the foaming shampoo. He blows his nose in his fingers, cleaning out one nostril at a time. He makes himself wheeze and cough, bring up phlegm from his chest and throat and spitting it onto the shower floor. He watches it swirling down the drain. Then he soaps his hands and scrubs them clean, using a nail brush to remove any specks of grease or dirt. He turns off the shower and shakes the excess water from his head. He moves his hands down his body to flick away any water that has collected in the hairs on his stomach, his backside, his legs. He steps out of the shower and rubs himself dry. He fixes the towel around his waist and looks at himself in the misty mirror. He cleans his teeth and combs his hair to slick and smooth perfection.

Then he goes back to his room and gets dressed. He pulls on a pair of freshly washed jeans. They are tight across the arse and cling to his thighs. He has carefully patched them with a strange assortment of symbols and signs. On his knee is sign that say 'Stop!', but the sign is a lie because further up, across his penis, he has sewn on another patch. This patch is a teapot with a provocative spout. On the teapot are printed the words, 'Rub me.'

HUNTING

Jonathan springs out of the boarding-house front door, whistling and carefree, jauntily twirling his car keys, striding down the front path and out to his big old tank of a car. He eases his tight arse into the driver's seat, spreads his legs wide, turns the car radio on and twiddles the dial until he finds a heavy rock beat, lights a cigarette, rests his right arm nonchalantly out of the window and rattles off down the street.

He drives slowly, eyes loitering along the footpaths. Jonathan is hunting but he is not sure what he is looking for. His sexual tastes are broad-based and all-embracing. His periods of incarceration in all male institutions have taught him to appreciate the ecstasies of a hot, hard cock. His experiences with women, during his brief spells of freedom, have taught him that all cunts are desirable. He has no particular predilection for old men or young boys, but, apart from these few exceptions, all human beings have the power to entice him. Sexuality is his essence.

As Jonathan drives along he finds himself travelling beside a familiar park. He is suddenly assaulted by a compulsion that he has felt many times before. His hands and legs want him to stop the car but he refuses to allow them to win and he forces himself to drive on. He is sweating now and his hands grip the wheel. He stops the car and goes into a milk bar and buys himself a can of Coke. He rolls himself a cigarette and makes himself sit down and smoke his cigarette and drink his Coke.

But the idea of what he must do is gathering impetus, growling black and rumbling in his mind and he goes over to the juke box and puts on a record in the hope that the music will drown out the tantalizing whisperings but the music is powerless and the whispering becomes a shrieking inside his skull and his legs get up and walk him to the car and his hands take the wheel and drive him to the place where he has to go and his mind surrenders to the compelling demand.

Jonathan drives back to the park and stops the car. He gets out and walks across the grass. He keeps walking until he reaches the Ladies' toilet. By now his palms are perspiring and his shirt is wet and his cock is hard inside his tight jeans. He looks around, hoping that he will not be seen. He knows that he should not do the thing he is about to do. He knows that he could easily be caught and that if he is caught he will end up in prison. Compulsion is stronger than reason and he goes on. He can feel the bile rise in his throat as he wonders if the toilets will be empty.

He goes inside. There are three cubicles. He is lucky this time; they are all empty. He goes into the middle cubicle and locks the door. Then he stands up on the toilet seat. He is in a good position now to look over into the toilets on either side.

He pulls down his pants and takes hold of his hard cock and waits. Five minutes go by. He can feel a tense excitement waiting in every muscle of his body. He hears footsteps dragging along the path. He can hear harsh breathing and sighs as the woman slowly enters the toilet. She goes into the cubicle on his right. He looks over, rubbing his cock at the same time. Mixed with desire is the terror that she might look up and see him peering at her. She is old and fat and wide and she puffs and pants as she struggles to lift her skirt, to pull down her pants, to stiffly ease herself onto the lavatory seat. He comes closer and closer to climax as he waits to hear the sound of her urine hitting the water at the bottom of the toilet. At last he hears and feels and smells the hot stream of her pee and the sound triggers his release to noiseless orgasm.

Now the horror of his compulsion envelops him. What if she has heard him? What if she screams? What if she cries, 'Help! Help! There's a man in the toilets!' He squats, cringing and shivering on the toilet seat, sickened by what he has done, promising that he will never, never, never do such a thing again. He is crying now; silent, tears run into his hands and down between his fingers.

He hears her pull the chain, struggle with her clothes, collect her things, leave the cubicle. She takes a long time to wash and dry her hands, to do her hair. The stale smell of urine makes him want to vomit. He swallows hard.

At last she leaves. He must wait a few more moments. He listens to the sound of her receding footsteps. Then he gets down off the toilet and zips up his trousers. The sound of his own frantic heartbeat deafens him as he swiftly slips outside again. No one sees him. He goes into the men's toilets and washes his face and hands.

Jonathan walks back across the grass. He gets into his car and drives away.

THE HOUSE NEEDS PAINTING

Eve and the house were synonymous – orderly and well-kept on the inside but showing signs of age on the outside.

Eve had become aware of her mortality. She woke each morning hugged by the greyness of her own death. She did not sense death in terms of its imminence but she felt the oppression of its inevitability. She saw it in the lankness of her once vibrant hair, noticed it in the prominent veins and creased skin of her hands, observed it in the discoloration of her teeth and the slight receding of her gums, felt it creep into the corners of her eyes and mouth. Death. She could not shrug it off.

She saw the natural processes of her own decay and realized that she was powerless to allay them but she wanted to do something to shake off the heaviness that seemed to accompany this recent recognition of her physical vulnerability.

She went out into the sunshine and had a good look at her house. She walked right around it, examining it carefully. When she had finished her inspection she said to herself, 'The house needs painting.'

She could not rejuvenate herself but she could revitalize her house.

Having come to this decision, Eve went inside and picked up the local newspaper. She looked through the Tradesmen columns until her eye stopped at the following advertisement:

PAINTER

Reliable, hard-working young man. No job too small.
Reasonable rates. Phone Jonathan – 806 3712

Eve knew that if she was going to get the house painted then she would have to arrange for it immediately. Although it was Sunday morning, she decided to go and ring up the painter.

Eve felt apprehensive at the prospect of having to use a telephone. She felt anxiety edging through her as she picked up her bag and left the house and walked to the telephone box at the corner of the street. She entered the box and picked up the receiver. She noticed that her palm was sweating so she took out a handkerchief and wiped her hands. Then she inserted her money and dialed Jonathan's telephone number.

Jonathan was, at this moment, masturbating in a ladies' toilet, but Eve was not to know that and she felt distressed and impatient as she waited for someone to answer the boarding house phone. Finally someone answered, took down her name and address and told her that Jonathan would contact her the next day.

Eve's legs felt shaky and her stomach fluttered as she left the telephone box and walked back to her house. She went straight into the lounge-room and sat down in an armchair. She let her eyes absorb the room, allowing the gentle cinnamon tones of the carpet and the curtains seep into her. She sat perfectly still and her hands hung motionless. Soon she could feel a calmness growing in her fingertips and spreading through her until she and the chair and the room were one. Then she closed her eyes and let herself merge into her surroundings. Only then could she permit her mouth to curve into the smallest smile.

EVE SHOULD HAVE BOUGHT A LADDER

Eve should have bought a ladder and painted the house herself. Not that Jonathan was a bad painter. He was quite a good one and he painted the house very carefully and very well. But Eve had opened the slightest gap in her armour.

She found herself making him cups of tea at lunch-time and listening to his mindless chatter while he ate his sandwiches and drank his tea at her kitchen table. She kept herself busy in the kitchen while he was there and did not allow herself to sit down with him but his endless monologue penetrated a part of her that she had shut off long ago. She gained possession of a basic array of facts: his father had died when he was young; he had spent a year of his childhood in hospital suffering from tuberculosis; he adored his mother but he'd been such a bastard that she had disowned him; he had a little sister about Ruth's age; he'd been imprisoned for stealing cars and breaking and entering; he'd spent as much time inside jail as outside it in the last six years; he'd decided to go straight and so had come to a new town to make a new start; he was never, never, never going back into prison again; he loved pop music and fast cars, dancing and home-cooked meals.

He was charming and gay and had a flair for telling stories. Sometimes his disarming anecdotes made her want to laugh. Sometimes, when he spoke of his mother and sister, he made her want to cry.

He would finish his painting for the day just as Ruth was coming home from school. He would go down the path to meet her as she came in the front gate and Eve would watch them through the lounge-room window. She could not hear their conversation but there was a joyous innocence in their coming together, an exuberance in their laughter and smiles.

At various times Jonathan tried to puncture Eve's defences. He asked her questions about the past, wanted to know why she and Ruth lived alone. She discouraged his questions by ignoring them, a mode of behaviour that he found both disconcerting and challenging. Jonathan believed that there was no woman on earth that he could not crack once he had decided to do so.

He noticed that, if he worked hard at it, he could get her to smile just a little and, although she pretended indifference, he could tell that she was ready to pity him.

Jonathan very much wanted to belong somewhere.

By the end of the week, when the painting was almost finished, he felt ready to make his request. Eve and Ruth were in the kitchen and he went in to them. He did not lead up to it in a gentle fashion but brought it out abruptly and directly.

'How about taking me on as a boarder,' he said. 'Let me rent that spare room of yours.'

Eve felt herself withdraw and knew that an immediate refusal was essential. She had an instantaneous 'No' ready but part of her hesitated and she found herself looking at Ruth. Ruth's eyes begged her mother to agree and, before Eve could do anything about it, she found that 'Yes' was rising in her throat and tumbling out of her mouth.

INNOCENCE

And so the three dwell in innocence. And it seems as if the long summer days hum between them and the soft nights lull and cradle them to sleep.

Ruth uncurls and curves beneath their ever watchful eyes. Her black hair gleams beneath the slanting sun and she turns her head this way and that to catch the mirrored beaming glow that flows from Eve and Jonathan.

Ruth rests secure. She is the axis of their earth and they are her fixed poles. She pivots and sways between them but they are moored, docked immobile at her either side.

JONATHAN

Jonathan expands. He blooms and grows.

He mows the lawns and trims the edges. Morning and evening he waters the summer-dry grass and the sun-baked flower beds. He clears a shady part of the garden and begins to establish a vegetable patch. He plants tiny carrots and green beans, tomatoes and radishes. He tends his precious seedlings with patient care and they respond with a surge of sturdy life.

His help is not restricted to the outside of the house. He washes the dishes each night after dinner. He takes out the garbage. He mends anything that breaks. He does everything he can to make himself indispensable.

And he radiates with the glow of belonging. The joy of being accepted illuminates him and it seems to Eve and Ruth that when he moves he scatters behind him a sparkling trail of sunlight.

His happiness bubbles into them and they are made light and buoyant as they glide on the wings of his exuberance.

AFTER YEARS OF THIRST

If only it were possible to stop here; to remain static, unmoved and unmoving, held in their harmony; to put down the pen and take up a camera instead; to focus in on them and click them to permanent immobility.

But the action cannot stop. Jonathan will not allow it. After years of thirst he has come upon a clear stream and he must bend his head and drink his fill.

Jonathan is not satisfied with the position he now holds in the lives of Eve and Ruth. He is driven by an aching need to entrench himself in their existence. And Jonathan's intuition tells him that there is only one way to achieve this desire. He knows he must move with care and caution. He knows he must utilize all the skill and expertise that he can summon. He knows that, if he is not extremely careful, his effort to gain ground could result in defeat.

He looks at his situation in a clear-sighted manner and decides, quite understandably, that he should take on the younger woman first. With patience and determination, he sets himself the task of seducing Ruth.

THE SEDUCTION BEGINS

Jonathan begins the seduction of Ruth by refusing to touch her. He draws around himself an invisible, inviolable area of taboo. Whenever they pass each other in the hallway, he presses himself against the wall so that there is no possibility of contact. He sits next to her at the breakfast table, but deliberately moves his chair just a few inches away from her. She comes into his room to listen to music but when she sits down on the bed next to him, he gets up and stretches himself out on the floor. He goes to the beach with her but keeps a defined distance between them and he no longer plays rough and tumble games with her in the sea. Ruth does not know why Jonathan's behaviour towards her has changed but she feels the power of the barricade that he erects between them.

Having established an immutable physical separation, Jonathan now proceeds with the second step of the seduction. He constantly seeks Ruth's company and, whenever he is with her, plays the role of devoted attendant. He looks at her and he talks to her and he captures her with his open gaze and his flowing words. He watches her swim in the stream of his eyes, flounder in the ocean of his voice.

Ruth feels that she will sink and drown. She longs to stretch out her hand, to touch, to hold. She wants him to clasp her hands, to grasp her, to pull her naked and wet from the pounding sea.

Then her days become a frenzy of flashing heat and shuddering cold, dry mouth and jelly limbs, aching lips and soundless sighs. He is her knight as he saves her from impending doom, armoured and shining in the dazzling sun, scooping to save her from the burning fires, racing her wild to the ends of the earth.

In her dark self she devours him whole, swallowing him in gulping, greedy mouthfuls. As she feeds on him her hunger mounts; it swells and roars and screams, black and urgent through her restless core.

But she stays within her boundaries, keeps her turmoil leashed and self-contained, maintains an external appearance of repose. She would like to question Jonathan, but she does not dare. She is aware that rules have been set down. She understands, intuitively, exactly what these rules are and she knows that she will have to obey them.

A RAINY AFTERNOON

On a rainy afternoon, in the moist summer heat, Jonathan takes Ruth to the movies. They are both wearing shorts and singlets and their brown limbs rest quietly, side by side, on the soft velvet seats. The lights dim and the theatre feels cool and still. The movie begins and Jonathan slumps down in his seat, to make himself more comfortable. As he does so, he makes sure that his bare shoulder and upper arm come in contact with hers.

Ruth is startled. The touch triggers a shock that blasts her calm and sends desire rioting through her, blocking out the images on the movie screen. She sits very still. She is sure that he will move away from her as soon as he realizes that they are touching. She waits. Why doesn't he move? The moment gapes and widens. It spreads and grows. She is trapped in timelessness.

She watches the film. She keeps her eyes on the actors and she hears the sound of their voices but their words and their actions are meaningless to her. Her real attention is focused on the few inches of skin that are touching Jonathan. She telescopes herself into that small patch of skin.

Here she hovers for a moment in her own flame and then she burns through herself and into him. She cannot stop. She sears through his flesh until she feels his life stream and then she penetrates its wall and enters his flow and she flares and blazes her way through his being.

Ruth is grateful that Jonathan is unaware of their union. He watches the movie and laughs with gusto but he is not really laughing at the film. What delights him is his awareness of what is happening to the girl beside him. He vibrates with the joy of his power.

At the end of the movie, Jonathan gets up abruptly and snaps their contact. He immediately re-establishes the prescribed distance between them and walks out of the theatre. Ruth follows him. There is nothing else that she can do.

WAITING

Jonathan waits for one week before he embarks on the last step of the seduction. He is aloof. He goes out each night, nicely dressed and neatly groomed. Ruth thinks that he has found another life in which there is no place for her. She does not know that he is, in fact, quite friendless and that he simply fills in the empty evenings by cruising up and down in his car, or going to the movies alone.

She feels what he intends her to feel – jealous, rejected, confused. She is ensnared by an ecstasy that swirls and encircles her. She is enmeshed in a frenzy that finds nowhere to go.

Jonathan commands her daydreams. He is her groom as she floats bejewelled and billowing in her white wedding gown. He is her Prince as he carries her, grateful-eyed, to his wide, silken bed. His lips touch hers and she forges life into the fantasied kiss. Her body begs for what should follow but she is foiled by her own innocence. She holds her longing in her hand and feels her suffering seep through her fingertips while fierce tears release themselves unexpectedly from her eyes.

THE LAST STEP

The week is over. An evening breeze slips through the house, lifting away the heat of the day. Ruth and Eve and Jonathan have just finished their meal. Jonathan is telling an amusing story about some childhood misdemeanor. His way of telling a story delights his listeners and they laugh with him as he recalls his early exploits.

When the story comes to an end, Jonathan looks at Ruth, puts on a charming smile, and asks her if she would like to listen to some music with him.

He leads the way into his room and closes the door. He puts on a record. He chooses one that he considers to be suitably stirring and romantic. Ruth curls up on the end of the bed. He sits down beside her and lights a cigarette. He rests his back against the wall and pretends to listen to the music.

Ruth does not move. He finishes his cigarette and stubs it out. Head back, eyes closed. Motionless. The record comes to an end. He gets up, turns the record over and puts on the other side. He sits down again on the bed.

As the music begins to play, he bends over Ruth and kisses her. She does not move. He kisses her softly and gently – on the lips, the cheeks, the forehead, the neck; along her arms, her hands, her fingertips. She lies still, permitting. He kisses her toes, her ankles, her calves, her knees, her thighs. He puts his hand under her dress and runs it across her stomach. He tries to lift her dress up and she moves and stretches out and arches her buttocks off the bed to make it easier for him to raise her dress and he lets it fall around her neck. His fingers touch her breasts, delicately cupping, softly squeezing, lightly rubbing. His lips close on her nipples and his tongue darts out to taste. She lies there. He rolls down her pants and again she raises herself to make his task easier, lifting first one thigh and then the other as he dexterously removes them, one-handed. His hand now hugs her cunt and his other hand removes her dress. She helps him by lifting her neck.

Her eyes are closed. He begins to stimulate her clitoris with his thumb. He starts slowly and gradually increases rhythm and pace. As he senses her excitement, he places his third finger on the outside of the entrance to her vagina and presses firmly. His finger tentatively inches its way into her vagina, the rhythm of the thumb on the clitoris never ceasing. He moves his finger further into her vagina until it meets the barrier of her hymen. She gives a momentary, sharp gasp as he forces his finger through and she sighs as he breaks into her and allows his finger to penetrate the inner recesses. He is holding her, kissing her, nuzzling her breasts while his right hand works below in relentless rhythm. He slows his hand down and he feels her yearning need so he speeds up the rhythm again. With absolute precision his finger thrusts in and out, in and out until he senses her nearness to orgasm and the final, forceful thrust of his finger brings her to a climax. He covers her with kisses and brings her gently back to the bed and to the room and to himself. He takes away his hand and picks up a towel. He wipes the bloody wetness from his hand and then, with apparent tenderness, wipes her clean.

He gets up and goes to the record player. He turns the record over and puts the first side back on again. He takes off his clothes. He lies down naked beside her. He begins again – to fondle, to touch, to kiss, to caress, to stimulate, to excite. This time, however, when he senses that she is ready, he carefully inserts his penis into her vagina. Once he is inside her, he moves as slowly and as gently as he possibly can and he makes quite sure that she reaches a climax before he allows himself to have one.

Not a word spoken.

EVE'S REACTION

It would be reasonable to suppose that Eve immediately observed a change in Ruth; that she perceived at once that Jonathan had seduced her daughter; that she hurled him out of the house in a mountain of maternal rage.

But Eve noticed nothing at all. Eve's personal method of human survival made it necessary for her to sidle through life with blinkers on. Eve was expert at blocking out anything she did not wish to see.

THE SEDUCTION OF EVE

The seduction of Eve is sharp and swift. It occurs a few days later, in the early afternoon, while Ruth is still at school. Jonathan comes home unexpectedly. He walks up to Eve and fastens her in his arms. She is undone in an instant. They claw off their clothes and hard and fast and fierce they fight their way to violent union.

HOW JONATHAN FEELS

Jonathan would like to jump and run and shout and leap. He would like to stand astride the globe and bellow out his victory. He would like to let his laughter roar and roll from mountain top to mountain top, to declare from high the power of the prick. God of the penis, riding bareback across the fields, trampling the tender earth beneath his thundering feet.

But he cannot proclaim his prowess. He becomes the tom cat on the nightly prowl, sneaking along the hallway, pussy-footing from room to room.

HOW EVE FEELS

Eve feels nothing at all. Her capacity for defending herself against intrusion enables her to believe that no intrusion has occurred. She refuses to admit that Jonathan has evoked a sexual response that has been lifeless for sixteen years. She allows him to enter her bedroom late each night and she allows him to enter her body. But as soon as he enters her she removes herself. She steps outside her body and crosses the room and stands by the window looking out into the night. She abandons her body and leaves it on the bed – unpatrolled, unsupervised, unleashed. Though Jonathan speaks to her as he makes love to her she does not listen to what he is saying. She doesn't even hear him. She certainly never answers him.

HOW RUTH FEELS

Ruth's ignorance and innocence combine to swathe her in the delusion of being loved. She gives herself to love with the frankness of her youth and inexperience. She dreams of a cottage and a primrose path, of holding Jonathan's hand along silver highways that surge up towards castles in the sky. She does not question. She does not ask. She assumes that love is both reciprocal and eternal.

ECSTASY

Jonathan has achieved what he set out to achieve, yet it brings him only momentary satisfaction. Ruth is no problem. He is able to set aside her desire to marry him by telling her that she is far too young for marriage and that, if she still loves him and wants to marry him in five years' time, he will most certainly marry her but meanwhile they must take precautions to prevent her from becoming pregnant. It is not difficult for Jonathan to make such promises. No, Ruth is no problem at all.

Jonathan's problem is Eve. Jonathan very rapidly becomes obsessed with Eve. Her alienation infuriates him. He wants to possess her, but succeeds only in occupying her body. He deliberately prolongs their love making, willing his penis to remain erect, refusing to climax. He wants to be fused with her forever and her body continues to lust with his for as long as he can keep an erection. While their bodies are making love he feels that she is his. The moment it is over, he knows that she is not his. He begs for love, pleads, cajoles and cries, but she screens herself in silence and ignores his whispered words.

He wants to smash her mask with his fist, gouge out her eyes, slit her belly open and cut her cunt to shreds but his sexuality is trapped in hers and he constantly swings between aggression and desire.

She helps him to maintain this precarious balance by complying with any sexual demand. Sometimes he ties her to the bed and vents his hostility upon her. Sometimes he begs her to mount and master him. The taste of her lingers on his tongue and he is compelled to rush home in the middle of the day, to lie beside her on the bed, to lick and suck and eat her while she climaxes time after time, flooding his face, filling his mouth.

He takes her into the toilet and sits on the seat, his penis erect. He makes her sit on top of him, his penis inside her. He hugs her and holds her and fucks her and begs her to do what he wants. He cries and trembles and shakes as he feels the longed for heat of her urine pouring down his cock, over his balls, along his thighs. He gets into the empty bath tub and pulls her cunt onto his face and his tongue darts from clitoris to vagina to rectum until she yields to his yearning and allows her whole body to open over him. He gulps and swallows and drinks and drowns. It is ecstasy.

FLIRTING WITH DEATH

Jonathan is at trigger edge. This welding of fantasy and reality, this bonding of truth and dream, has shocked, numbed, dulled him. His reactions are unpredictable, his passions beyond control.

He thinks he has awakened Eve but her sexual emergence is not a metamorphosis into life. It is a shadowy flirtation with death. Murder lies beside her on the bed.

Enthralled, he follows her; enslaved, he worships her; helpless, he hovers in her tempting twilight.

MOTHER AND DAUGHTER

They are sitting at the breakfast table on a sunny Sunday morning. Mother and daughter. Nine o'clock. Jonathan is not awake yet. Soon Ruth will go and bang on his door, call out to him, make him wake up, remind him that it is Sunday and time for him to take her to the beach. It is her day. Every Sunday is her day, hers and Jonathan's. A time to be together, to swim and lie in the sun, to climb the rocks and run along the beach, to hold hands and lick ice-creams, to laugh and cuddle and kiss. She will give him another half hour to sleep. Meanwhile she sits at the kitchen table with her mother, drinking tea and flicking through the Sunday papers.

Ruth has become expert at appearing to be occupied. She has learned how to make her eyes move down the page at the correct speed. It has become necessary for Ruth to develop this skill because she wants to hide the fact that all her waking time is spent in day-dreaming. She dreams of love, of Jonathan, of happiness that will be. She cannot talk about her love to anyone. She senses that her mother would disapprove. Although some of her school friends go out with boys, they are not involved with men like Jonathan and she knows that she has reached a level of sexual experience that is, as yet, unknown to them. She keeps her relationship to herself.

So Ruth sits with her mother and pretends to be reading the Sunday papers. She stretches her right hand out on the table in front of her. She can feel that Eve can see the hand stretched out and she knows what will happen next. Eve continues to read her paper but allows her left hand to move slowly towards her daughter's. She touches Ruth's hand, gives it a gentle squeeze and then lets her hand remain there. A warm and companionable silence rests between them.

Then Eve's hand grasps her daughter's sharply and Ruth looks up into her mother's face to see what is wrong. Eve's face is taut, her lips stretched tight. Her back is rigid, her muscles tensed. She lets go of Ruth's hand and abruptly pushes herself up from the table. She rushes into the bathroom and Ruth can hear the harsh, gushing sound of her mother vomiting into the toilet.

THE SPECTATOR

Ruth becomes an observer, subjecting her mother and Jonathan to careful scrutiny. Her attention never leaves them. She strives to make her surveillance subtle but Eve and Jonathan are aware of her absorption in them and they veil themselves against her.

She is sitting with them now at the kitchen table. They are having a late evening cup of tea. She watches the way they sit, bodies tight and controlled. She slouches in her chair, affecting a relaxed pose, trying to counteract their strain. She sees how her mother's hand holds the teacup, fingers white and bloodless.

Something is going to explode. She thinks that if she ignores their tension, if she goes on pretending not to notice their anxiety, then everything will be all right.

The situation in the house has changed. She doesn't want it to have changed and she doesn't know why it has changed and she hopes that, if she can maintain the role of spectator, things might go back to the way they were.

Her separation from what is going on before her is so effective that she feels she is watching a drama unfolding on the stage. She cannot question the characters about what is wrong. She cannot ask the actors what will become of them. She can only watch and wait.

As she sits with them at the table she senses that they are waiting for her to go to bed but as they do not ask her to leave she stays where she is, sitting and waiting. She hopes that they will ignore her presence and, by their words and movements, help her to understand what is going on but they remain silent, sipping their tea. When the silence becomes intolerable they begin to talk on the level of civil niceties. She does not join in their polite talk but simply watches and listens.

Suddenly, Ruth cannot put up with the undercurrents that fly between them. She gets up and leaves the room. She goes into her bedroom and closes the door, loudly and purposefully. Then she quietly opens it a fraction of an inch in the hope that she might be able to hear what they say to each other. She undresses and gets into bed.

They remain silent and the heaviness of their no-words edges through the crack of her door and spreads over her. Then she hears their voices, soft, even and low. She can hear Eve talking, then Jonathan; then Eve, then Jonathan. They talk for a long time and the hum of their voices almost sends her to sleep. Now the voices change. Jonathan's voice rises hotly; Eve's becomes harsh and cold. Despite the rise in volume, Ruth still cannot distinguish the words but she tries to interpret their meaning by listening to the change in tone. Jonathan's voice fluctuates, rising and falling. It sounds like anger. It sounds like love. It begs and pleads. It shouts and screams.

Then she hears him stand, hears the chair scrape back, hears his open hand bang in anger on the kitchen table, hears him thumping down the hall, slamming the front door, roaring his car to a violent start, tyres screeching down the road.

Now her room seems quiet and dark and the darkness echoes her own emptiness. She wishes her mother would come into her room and sit on the bed, stretch out her hand in sweet caress. She wishes that there had never been a Jonathan. She longs for a return to the time when there had been just Eve and herself, mother and daughter, warm and secure.

She hears Eve get up and listens to her washing up the teacups, tidying the kitchen. She listens as her mother locks the back door, goes into the lounge room to make sure the windows are closed, turns off the lights and walks into the hall. She hears her go into the bathroom. The bathroom door closes. She can hear the sound of the shower running and she lies in the darkness, waiting for her mother to finish. She imagines that she is a little girl again, standing with Eve under the steaming shower heat. She lifts her baby arms and hugs the slippery skin, burying her head in Eve's warm belly. She can feel the water beating down on both of them, cleansing them as one. The sound of the shower stops and she waits while Eve dries herself. Soon the bathroom door will open and her mother will walk down the hall. She knows that, any moment now, Eve will come in, make sure she is covered, tuck her in, lightly brush her forehead with a kiss. She pretends to be asleep but her heart beats high as she awaits this needed touch of love.

The footsteps move down the hall but they do not stop. The footsteps do not even hesitate outside Ruth's door. Eve keeps walking. She goes into her own room and closes the door sharply.

Ruth lies still for a few moments then she curls up her legs, turns on to her side and pulls the covers lightly over her head. She can feel the fierce tears sliding sideways across her face.

THE ARGUMENT

Eve and Jonathan have been arguing about the baby that has begun to grow in Eve's womb.

Eve does not want to argue about the baby because, as far as Eve is concerned, Jonathan has nothing to do with the baby and the baby has nothing to do with Jonathan. She states, quite clearly, that the baby is hers alone and that she would be very happy if Jonathan found somewhere else to live as soon as possible.

Jonathan finds Eve's attitude incomprehensible. All that matters to Jonathan is that Eve is carrying his child. As far as he knows he has never fathered a child before and the fact that he has now done so fills him with pride and joy. He is somewhat surprised to find himself the victim of such conventional sentiments but he feels them, none the less, and he is determined to marry Eve. His desire to marry her is not based solely on the fact that he has made her pregnant. He wants to bind her to him in the same way as his body is enslaved to hers and he believes that marriage will achieve this.

Eve, of course, has no intention of marrying anyone and tells him so. He begs, he cajoles and pleads but his vows of eternal love have no effect on her. Now that she is pregnant, she wants to get rid of him. She finds, however, that getting rid of him is not going to be easy.

He says that he cannot, will not go, that he must stay with her forever. He tells her, quite calmly, that if she insists on his leaving then he will kill her. He will kill her and find a way to preserve her body. He will dress her up in exotic clothes and brush out her long, frizzy hair. He will decorate her with rings and bracelets and necklaces. He will lie her on a bed of black velvet and spread her hair out on the pillow. He will paint her face and burn incense sticks around her bed. He will lock her up in a room and come and fuck her whenever he feels like it. Then she will belong to him forever.

Then he shouts at her and screams at her and calls her bitch and whore. He pushes back his chair, gets up from the table, flings himself down the hall and slams his way out of the house.

Eve recognizes Jonathan's madness, believes in his potential for violent action. She feels an instinctive need to protect the child in her womb and this anxiety dominates her thoughts as she washes up the teacups and has a shower and gets herself into bed. For the first time in fifteen years, she forgets to go in and kiss her daughter goodnight.

A FEW HOURS LATER

A few hours later, Ruth is still lying awake. She has stopped crying but she is unable to sleep. She is trying to assess the significance of the argument between her mother and Jonathan. Her mind keeps flying from one interpretation to another. She knows that Jonathan's general messiness and untidiness irritate Eve; she hopes the argument might have been about that. She knows that Jonathan's loud playing of music disturbs Eve's peace and calm; perhaps they were arguing about that. She knows that Jonathan has been negligent in paying his rent; maybe that was the cause of the argument.

Although Ruth's mind keeps presenting her with such pragmatic explanations she knows that none of them is true. She has overheard voices powered by emotion, propelled by passion. Her mother's failure to kiss her goodnight signifies something ominous. The entwined image of her mother and Jonathan as lovers struggles darkly to break through but even a momentary glimpse of such a possibility is so horrific that Ruth cannot allow it to emerge. So she lies awake, struggling with the inexplicable.

Eve is also lying awake. She has locked her door but left her reading light on. She stares at her white walls and her white curtains and she pulls her white sheets tightly around her. She tries to relax, to let herself merge with the whiteness. It does not work. Jonathan has succeeded in puncturing her calmness and control. She lies awake, listening for his return.

Out of the silence Eve can hear a car speeding down her street. She hopes that it will pass by but it slams to an abrupt and noisy halt outside her house. She hears Jonathan striding up the path, his key turning in the lock. She snaps out her light.

His footsteps move firmly down the hall and stop outside her door. He taps gently. She does not answer. He turns the handle of the door and she can sense his irritation at finding it locked. He taps more sharply. She remains still and quiet.

He is angry now and calls to her to unlock the door. She does not move. He bangs his fists in fury on the door, hammering and shouting, warning her that if she doesn't open the door he will smash it down.

Eve puts on the light and gets up and unlocks the door. Jonathan shoves his way in, grabs her with both hands and shakes her roughly. Then he pushes her down onto the bed and keeps her trapped there with one of his hands and the weight of his body. With the other hand he unzips his trousers but then he senses her passivity and he lets her go long enough to undress himself. He pulls off her nightdress and forces her legs apart. He plunges his penis into her with swift, vicious thrusts and as he takes her he curses her, calling her bitch and cunt and whore. She lies quite still, neither responding nor resisting.

And when he is finished he begins to moan and weep. He cries his love in tears that flow from him to her to the bed until the pillow and the sheets are soaked in his sorrow. His body shakes in great, ungovernable sobs and she begins to soothe and stroke, to murmur and caress and he is calmed by her soft mother touch and he lies quiet inside her, hushed and spent.

Ruth can hear Jonathan shout and curse, grunt and thrust, sob and cry. She can hear it all and she would like to go to her mother's aid but she is pinned to her bed, immobilized by fear. As Jonathan quietens down she can feel the rigidity leaving her limbs. Now she can move in the bed, breathe more regularly, fell less afraid.

At first the silence is soothing but then the stillness weaves itself around her, permeates her, urges her to get up, to find out what has happened. It is hard to get up, almost impossible. She must struggle against the unknown ties that bind her to her ignorance before she is finally able to wrench herself from the bed.

She moves slowly out of her room and stands in the dark hall, looking into her mother's room. She can see her mother lying on the bed. Jonathan is lying on top of her. They are both naked and absolutely still. She is certain that they are dead.

She does not know how long it is that she stands like this at the doorway, stunned and staring. She feels detached yet compelled to keep her eyes on the figures on the bed. She notices how Eve's reading light casts half shadows across their nakedness.

As she watches she imagines she can see slight movements from the bodies on the bed. Jonathan's body seems to press more firmly into Eve's; Eve's arms appear to tighten more securely around Jonathan. They begin to move with a gentle, almost imperceptible, rhythm. His face nudges and nuzzles into hers. Their heads move slightly so that their lips can meet and she can see their tongues touch, lips linger in soft, slow caress. Their bodies rock in rhythm and Ruth begins to feel her body sway with theirs. Ruth can sense the moment when his penis swells, can feel its length unfold inside her mother. She watches, enthralled, and yearns to make herself a part of their union. She longs to tear them apart, to slide in between them, to sink under them, to share their oneness. She must pull off her nightdress and rush to the bed. She hurls herself onto them and hugs her legs around them and abandons herself to the tumult of their ecstasy.

REACTIONS

Reactions are slow in shaping. They cannot look at one another. They untwine themselves and move apart as if the touch of one another's bodies has become odious. Ruth moves to one edge of the bed and turns away. Jonathan lies on his back, in the centre. Eve rolls to the other side. Potent taboos spring swiftly into place, filling all the empty spaces on the bed.

Ruth's throat is filled with filth and abomination. She would like to cry out but she knows that if she opens her mouth a torrent of vile, nauseous bile will burst out of her.

Eve withdraws, retreats to the safe walls of her own internal fortress, unwilling and unable to look at what has happened.

Jonathan stares at the ceiling. He takes stock of his situation, chews it over, examines it carefully, lets it roll around for a while inside his skull. His lips start to smirk and smile; involuntary sniggers and giggles escape from his mouth; unwitting chuckles and chortles rise and emerge until his body begins to shake with wild, unbridled bouts of laughter.

His laughter breaks the barriers between them and first Ruth, then Eve, turn towards him, amazed at his reaction. Small smiles begin to hover in their eyes, come unbidden to their lips. Unwillingly they join in his rejoicing. He puts an arm around each of them and draws them firmly to him. At this moment, Jonathan is sure that he has won.

EXPLORING POSSIBILITIES

For the three people in the bed, the world stands still. Ruth stops going to school. Jonathan stops going to work. Eve stops tidying the house.

They speak scarcely at all yet they are hurtling together into space, discovering new galaxies, uncovering unexplored wonders in a world where old laws are irrelevant and new patterns must be forged.

They spend much of their time on Eve's bed, slowly examining the possibilities of their three-fold union.

Jonathan sees himself as the axis of the relationship. He is the powerful pivot, the catalyst of their actions and reactions. He assumes responsibility and directs their activities. He longs to be smothered in female flesh, to drown beneath their sensuality and he loves to pull the women down upon him and lose himself beneath them. They are willing to satisfy his wants and he, in turn, is always able to arouse and gratify their intense desires.

As they become more accustomed to their triple fusion Jonathan instigates a shift in emphasis. He gives up the centre place and, instead, places Ruth in the middle of the bed. He can sense, in Eve, a hammering of hidden fantasies and he encourages her to unleash them.

He lies beside Ruth and runs his hands gently over her breasts, her stomach, her thighs. He takes Eve's hand and places it on Ruth's face. Ruth wants to move away from her mother's touch but Jonathan is insistent and she lets her mother stroke her forehead, allows Eve's fingers to linger around her eyes and cheeks, chin and neck. Ruth succumbs to the joy of being the object of their loving and she closes her eyes and gives herself up to their tender touch. Eve and

Jonathan become indistinguishable as they both seek to cover her with caresses. Hands and lips flutter across her skin. She can feel them weave around her as they vie with each other to delight and arouse her. Hands press her breasts, tongues take her nipples, lips kiss her thighs. A face nudges up between her legs and she can feel an eager tongue tentatively touch her clitoris. The tongue explores, tastes, savours, slides into her. It teases and torments, penetrating, then moving away. She is wet with wanting and arches herself for the tongue's return, her body begging it to stay. The tongue is ravenous now, demanding satisfaction. Ruth hesitates for a moment and holds back but the mouth insists. Ruth lets herself rise and glide, soar and fly. Her body tightens and contracts as she reaches her peak and then explodes as she pours down upon the urgent mouth the orgasm that it requires.

Silence. Stillness. Tears at the corners of her eyes. Ruth has never been on a journey such as this. She is reluctant to return. Unwillingly she comes back to the house and to the room and to the bed. The head that belongs to the mouth is resting on her belly. Ruth knows that if she opens her eyes and looks down at the head, she will be gazing into the face of her mother.

FUSION

Too late for logic. Too late for reason. Too late for sanity. It is only possible to turn back, unscarred, from the realm of dream and fantasy. Once it is real, there is no turning back. Once the fences of convention have been trampled down, they can never be erected again. They must remain, shattered and splintered, at one's feet.

So it is for Ruth and Eve and Jonathan. They have freed themselves of all restraints and yet the overriding feeling is not of liberation but of bondage. They are joined to one another, tied to one another, bound to one another.

Within the boundaries of the bed they are safe and sure. They know, with certainty, what is and what can be. Here is a world of unceasing lust. Passion sparks passion in continuous circuit. Yet the circuit is closed, restricted and confined.

They are unwilling and unable to separate. Everything must be done in unison. They must go to the bathroom together to shower or to wash. They must go to the kitchen together to prepare and eat their meals. When they run out of food they must go together to buy more. They must hold one another's hands as they do their shopping in order to keep the cord of their oneness intact. They can feel the hostile stares of an outside and alien world but they make themselves invulnerable by clinging together. It is a time of total fusion.

THERE WOULD BE NO TRAGEDY

If it were possible for human beings to live in such conjunction, to remain harmonious and secure, entwined and entrenched in one another's souls, then the three of them could be left in Eve's bed, merged forever.

If that were possible, there would be no tragedy.

EVE

Eve is the one to break the circle. She begins to feel suffocated. She wants to be alone again, to withdraw inside herself, to focus her attention on the baby that is developing in her womb.

She wakes up one morning and looks at the two people who are sharing her bed. A cool hatred spreads through her and she is repelled by their proximity. She gets out of bed and shakes them awake. She orders Ruth to get up and to shower and dress for school. She insists that Jonathan get himself ready to go out and look for work.

Ruth and Jonathan are stunned by her roughness. They are so shocked, so fragmented and disordered by her splitting of their bonds that they are, for the moment, unable to assess what is happening. Her insistence is so forthright that it renders them helpless. They obey her commands.

When Eve has got rid of them, she goes back into her bedroom. She strips the bed, turns the mattress, shakes the pillows, opens the windows wide and vacuums the floor. She gets a bucket of hot, soapy water and washes the bed-head, the bedside tables and the woodwork on the base of the bed. She removes from the bedroom anything that belongs to either Ruth or Jonathan. She sprays the room with air-freshener and makes up a clean, white bed. She goes out of her room and closes the door. She is determined that no one but herself will ever enter the room again.

Then she starts on the bathroom, cleaning the hand-basin, the toilet, the shower and the bath, scrubbing the floor with vigorous zeal. Next comes the kitchen. She tidies the bench tops, clears the kitchen table, washes down the cupboards, cleans out the fridge. She moves from room to room until the whole house is cleansed. Then she goes outside and mows the lawn, washes the windows, scours the front steps and polishes the door-knob. Satisfied, she goes back inside. She takes off her dirty clothes, has a long shower, washes her hair and cleans her teeth. By the end if the day she has resumed her meticulous mask.

RUTH

Ruth does not have Eve's means of disguising herself. As she walks down the street, on her way to school, she feels she has been peeled raw. She knows that her clothes are covering her, but she feels naked. The early autumn breeze whips into her, confirming her feeling that her skin and clothes are nothing more than layers of transparency.

The prospect of school is cold and frightening. Everyone will be able to look into her and see what has happened to her. Her legs and hands shake; her face feels pale. She recalls Eve's bed and the memory pulls at her, envelops her.

She cannot go to school and she cannot go home so she keeps walking until she finds herself in the park. She selects a sheltered, sunny spot and sits down, her back against a tree. She closes her eyes and lifts her face to the sun, hoping that its warmth might calm and soothe her. The random patterns that illuminate the darkness behind her eyes mirror the chaos of her thoughts.

Out of her disorder, swift, sharp stabs of hate burn their way fiercely to the surface. Hatred of Eve. To be rejected; to be dismissed; to be torn away from the heat of love. Intolerable. Unbearable.

She struggles away from the image of Eve and tries, instead, to conjure up Jonathan. Jonathan – husband of her dreams – all broken, smashed and gone. Hatred of Eve suffuses her again. She breaks away from the hate and forces herself to focus on Jonathan. She reminds herself that, although Eve has dismissed her daughter, she has also dismissed Jonathan. Ruth clutches at the possibility of regaining Jonathan's love. Such a thought is desirable, acceptable, even plausible. She holds onto it for as long as she can.

Then a twist cuts across her vision of normality. Jonathan wants Eve. Jonathan loves Eve. She has been a witness to his needs. Jealousy and hatred overpower her. She struggles for sanity. She must not let go of the thought that Eve has pushed Jonathan out of the bed. Eve has withdrawn her love and here is Ruth, young and desirable, willing and available. Surely she can win Jonathan's love. Soon Jonathan will realize that Eve is old and ugly. He will love Ruth and Ruth alone. And this time she will not share. With this point determined and firmly secured in her mind, Ruth is able to open her eyes. She will go back to school tomorrow. For the moment, it is sufficient to have found a way to face her world.

She has nowhere to go so she stays where she is, allowing herself to merge with the breeze and the sun, the birds and the trees. Calm now. Content. Secure.

She lets her eyes wander idly over the park and, in the distance, she observes a man walking across the grass. As he gets closer she can see that the man is Jonathan. She would like to signal him, to wave or call out, but her thoughts have exhausted her and she is, as yet, too worn out to make a move.

She watches him turn towards the toilets and she tells herself that, when he comes out, she will get up and go to him. She keeps her eyes on him. He is moving quickly now, almost running. When he reaches the toilet block she is somewhat puzzled by the fact that he enters the side marked 'Ladies'.

JONATHAN

When Eve ordered Jonathan out of bed and out of the house, Jonathan knew that she meant exactly what she said. He could see a tightness in her lips and an iciness in her eyes and he knew, in an instant, that he had lost. Last time he had resorted to threats and violence in order to win her back but one look at her told him that it would not work again. Now Eve looked at him as if she wanted him to be dead.

He pulled on his clothes and left the house but could no more look for a job than Ruth could go back to school so he drove around in his car for a while trying to sort out what he was going to do.

He tried to tell himself that Eve was just another cunt, that he could easily forget her. All he had to do was drive off, leave town, go somewhere else and start again. Plenty more women in the world. No need to stick around and be ordered about by this one. No bitch of a woman was going to tell him what to do. Yes, that's what he'd do. Go off and forget all about her. Wouldn't even bother to go back for his belongings. Just drive off to another town. So he lit a cigarette, turned the radio up loud, eased his elbow out of the window and raced off down the highway.

After he had been driving for about an hour he pulled up at a service station to fill his car with petrol. He bought himself a can of Coke and stood in the sun to drink it. While he was standing there he started to cry. He lifted his hand and tried to wipe the tears away but they kept coming and his body started to shake with heaving sobs. Eve and her baby crowded up inside of him. They were all that mattered to him. He threw away his empty can, jumped into his car and headed back to the town. Whatever she said, whatever she did, he belonged to Eve and the baby. He would never be able to leave them.

He kept sobbing and weeping. He wanted to go straight to Eve's house and fall down at her feet but he didn't dare. She had told him to look for work and he could not go back to her until later in the day. He felt disordered and distraught. Then he began to feel the dark beginning of a familiar urge. He moaned as he felt his compulsion overtake him. He cursed Eve. If she had not thrown him out of the bed, he would not have to do this. He headed his car in the direction of the park.

When he got there he pulled up, got out, slammed the car door and set off across the park towards the toilets. So urgent was his need that he had to walk quickly. The walk gave way to a run and he did not even look around to see if it was safe but plunged into the ladies' toilet and locked himself in the middle cubicle.

RUTH AND JONATHAN

Ruth waits for Jonathan to come out of the toilet. She waits for a long time. No one goes in. No one comes out. She begins to believe that she has been mistaken. Perhaps Jonathan is not there at all.

There are people in the park now. Mothers are sitting on park benches; small children are running in the early afternoon sunlight, laughing, rolling in the grass, trying to catch the elusive birds. Ruth observes them with detachment.

She is still reluctant to move. Her legs feel heavy and dull. She has been sitting still for so long that it requires great effort to get herself up. She walks slowly towards the toilet block and goes inside. She is apprehensive on entering, afraid of what she might find there. The toilets appear to be empty. The centre cubicle door is closed but Ruth bends down and looks under the door. She cannot see any feet on the floor. Jonathan is not there. She stands still.

It is very quiet.

She becomes aware of the nauseating smell, a mixture of staleness and disinfectant. She wants to turn around and walk straight out but she needs to urinate so she goes into the nearest cubicle, pulls down her pants and sits on the toilet. When the urine stars to flow she feels that it will never cease. It is as if all the uneasiness of the day is streaming out of her.

When she has finished she wipes herself, pulls up her pants, stands up and turns around to pull the chain. As her hand goes up to reach the chain, her eyes are drawn upwards and she find herself staring into the mad, distorted mask of Jonathan's face.

A scream gathers itself, forces its way into her throat and emerges from her mouth with a loud, reverberating cry. Jonathan gets down and grabs her, tries to quieten her but she cannot stop. Scream follows upon scream. There is no holding back.

Women rush to the toilet block, surround Ruth and Jonathan, pulling, clawing, demanding explanations. He is sweating with fear. He talks on and on. The girl's his friend; he is like a brother to her; he boards at her house; she has been upset lately, ill, unbalanced, disturbed; he is trying to help her. She had gone into the toilets; she had been there a long time; he had started to worry about her; he had gone in to find her; she had become hysterical. He had to get her home, get her into bed, get a doctor for her. They must let him go; he is just trying to help her. He keeps talking as he makes his way out of the toilets and the women part and let him by and he drags her, screaming still, across the park and into his car and the women watch and wonder as he starts his car and drives away.

Once out of sight of their prying eyes, he slows down the car and hits her hard across the face. The screaming stops. Ruth sits stunned. He begins to talk to her, softly, persuasively. He cannot help it; he is compelled to do such things; he has had a hard life, a bad start; the world has always been against him; no one has ever understood him.

Ruth looks out of the window. She knows that the words are there, flooding from him to her but she cannot let them in. She cannot even look at him. If she looks at him she will see again the monstrous vision of his face, peering at her over the lavatory wall.

He mistakes her stillness for calmness, her silence for understanding. There is no further need to speak. He drives quickly along the open road letting the cold wind dry his sweat and clear his head. When he considers the time to be right, he turns the car around and drives back to Eve's house.

Ruth gets out of the car and walks into the house. She goes straight to her room, takes off her clothes, changes into a pair of warm pyjamas and puts her bedsocks on. Then she gets into bed. She pulls the covers over herself and, as she does so, the thought occurs to her that she might just as well stay in bed forever.

AUTUMN

Ruth had been tampered with, interfered with, stained and torn beyond repair. She would like to die but she cannot die. Nor can she sew up the tattered remnants of herself. She continues to exist without any reason for existence.

Throughout the autumn she lives inside the house. She is unable to move outside its walls. She spends most of her time inside her room lying in her bed.

Jonathan feels some responsibility for her condition. He wills her to get well and helps by cooking her food, taking her to the bathroom, washing her, making her bed. She allows herself to be attended to but she does not recognize her attendant. Her eyes are wide and vacant. She is unresponsive and inert.

Eve is intolerant, almost indifferent to her daughter's plight. She feels no guilt. As far as Eve is concerned, the weeks of love-making never existed. She is engrossed in the new life that begins to stir and move inside her. Her fragmented daughter is an object of irritation. She would like to sweep up the pieces and hide them under the mat.

Jonathan behaves as she wants him to behave. He does not want to run the risk of her sending him away. He plays the willing slave. He must be satisfied to be near her and to watch the baby grow.

The house is silent most of the time. There is nothing left to say.

WINTER

Mid-winter. Bleak winds and heavy rains. The days are indistinguishable.

Eve and Jonathan are waiting while the baby grows. The baby is getting fat and large inside Eve's womb. Eve swells and glows. When Jonathan looks at her he feels illuminated by her light. She is precious and holy to him. She is carrying his child. Sometimes she allows him to put his hand on her belly and feel the baby kick and move. He is hushed with wonder and with awe. If only she would allow him more. He lives in the belief that she will, eventually, admit him to parenthood. He does not accept her view that the baby belongs to her alone.

Ruth is also waiting for something but whatever it is that she is waiting for lacks clear definition. She is still broken and detached but, as the months pass, a few shredded thoughts begin to merge together, forming dim patterns in her disordered mind. Something urges her to get up, to move out from the bed. She takes over one armchair in the loungeroom and spends most of her time sitting there. Though her eyes do not appear to see, she is, in fact, observing Eve.

She is constantly aware of the growing size of Eve's belly. She is fascinated and repelled by the way the baby has distorted her mother, making her features coarse and her body gross. Images flash of a slim, naked Eve – small breasts, sweet nipples, soft skin. A blaze of pain at such remembrances.

Winter passes. The baby continues to grow. Ruth sits and watches.

SPRING

It is springtime. A bright, sunny, Sunday morning. Eve is ready for the baby to be born. She is so heavy that she can barely move. Her small frame seems strained from the weight of the baby. She feels a dull, dragging pain across her pelvis. She knows that labour will begin soon and she decides to have a bath and get herself ready to go to the hospital.

Ruth sits in her armchair, listening. She can hear the bath-water running, hear the taps turn off, hear her mother step into the bath. She feels compelled to make some great effort, to get herself out of her chair, to go into the bathroom, to look at Eve in the bath.

Eve has left the bathroom door open and Ruth stands in the doorway. The baby floats high above the water line, moving and weaving under Eve's skin. It is so alive, so eager to get out that Ruth almost expects it to break its bonds and burst out of Eve's belly. Ruth stands there for a few minutes, absorbed, watching Eve and watching Eve's baby.

Then Ruth goes to the kitchen and takes out the carving knife. As soon as she grasps it in her hand she knows that she is fired with the power of angels and the strength of gods. She goes back into the bathroom.

Eve's eyes are closed. She is in pain and breathing sharply. The baby has stopped moving and has contracted itself into a high, rigid mound. Ruth moves swiftly to Eve and, with an iron left hand, forces Eve's head under the water. Her strong right arm plunges the knife into Eve's throat. She withdraws the knife and stabs it into Eve again and again, into her face, into her breasts, into her heart. She stops for a moment. She stares, fascinated, at the baby. It has started to move again. She lifts her knife and keeps stabbing until the baby is still.

Then she slits Eve's belly open and cuts away the sack that surrounds the baby. She lays down her knife and puts in her hands and pulls the baby out. She lifts it up and looks at it. She notes that it would have been a boy. She puts the baby back into the bathtub.

She can hear Jonathan walking up the hall. Jonathan stops in the doorway. He looks at Ruth and he looks at Eve and he looks at the baby. He stands still for a very long time.

Then a low wail comes out of his mouth and he stumbles over and kneels down beside the bath. His hands go out to Eve but he cannot make himself touch her and he grabs hold of the side of the bath instead and bends his head down and rests it on the edge. He starts bumping his forehead onto the bath, slowly, gently, despairingly, his body rocking with each bump. His body builds a mounting rhythm and he bangs his head, harder and harder, into the side of the bath. Soon his head is swinging in a brutal frenzy, pounding itself into the bath. A final, violent smash sends him sprawling to the floor.

Ruth steps out of pyjamas, runs some cold water in the handbasin and washes away the blood. She goes into her room and puts on a pair of jeans and a brightly coloured shirt. She brushes her hair and looks at herself in the mirror. Then she goes down the hall, opens the front door and walks out of the house.

NARCISSUS

JUDITH

Margaret's baby was born in Sydney in December, 1941. She arrived just in time for Christmas but she certainly didn't bring any joy with her. Margaret took one look at her and then turned her face to the wall. She was, admittedly, only nineteen years old and her husband, Joe, with whom she had spent a total of fifteen days of marital bliss, was away, no one knew where, fighting for Australia. Everyone said that explained why she turned her face to the wall.

Margaret had known she was pregnant, had seen her stomach grow, had felt the baby move and kick but had not been able to accommodate the notion that such physical occurrences would, inevitably, result in her becoming a mother. She was not ready to be a mother. She was not even ready to be a wife. When the birth started she did not go along with it. She tightened herself up and resisted what was happening in her womb. Consequently, the baby tore the unyielding flesh and Margaret had to be anaesthetized at the moment of birth and extensively stitched together again. They stitched up the sides of her vagina and they even had to stitch up a tear in her bowel. She was not permitted to get up for a week and she was definitely not allowed to shit. When they brought Margaret the baby, she didn't believe it was hers. Her body had been outraged and so she turned her face to the wall.

The doctors tried to cheer her up with injections and pills. The nurses tried to get her to accept the baby. The harder they tried, the less they succeeded. Margaret slammed down the shutters inside her skull. She wanted to die but they wouldn't let her. She refused food but they fed her intravenously. They tried to make her feed the baby but her nipples hardened and no milk flowed. They propped her up and tried to induce her to hold the baby but her arms opened and went rigid and the baby would have rolled off Margaret's lap and smashed onto the floor if a nurse hadn't snatched it up at the very last moment.

They didn't know what to do so they let her stay in the hospital for six weeks. By the end of that time they seemed to have convinced her that the baby was hers and that she would have to take it home and look after it. They insisted that the baby be given a name. Margaret couldn't think of one so the nurses chose Judith. It was not a very good start to life.

The Government Defence Department kept sending Margaret a large proportion of Joe's weekly wage so she didn't need to work. She put the baby in a bassinet in the second bedroom. She attended to it when necessary and left it alone the rest of the time. She never smiled at the baby and the baby never smiled at her. When the baby was four months old, Margaret got a job in a milk bar and she paid the woman next door to look after baby Judith while she was away.

Then Margaret started to feel alive again. She was not exactly common, but she was a brassy, almost vulgar-looking young woman with large breasts and wide hips. She liked the way the young boys looked at her as she fixed their chocolate malted milkshakes. She worked long hours and was happy to do overtime during weekends. She always stashed the money away and thought it would come in handy when Joe came back from the war, if he ever did come back. She liked to flirt, but there weren't many young men around and flirting was as far as she would go. She worked hard and waited for Joe.

Judith meanwhile, turned one, then two, then three, then four. She was adequately attended to by the woman next door, who was large and warm and smelled of milk and home-made bread. She had five children of her own and Judith fitted in where she could. She spent her days on the sidelines watching how a mother and five children loved and hated, kissed and cursed, hugged and hit, laughed and wept. They were lucky. The man of the family had, while a boy, been injured in an accident. He was unfit for army service but able to run the local garage and repair shop despite an obvious limp in his left leg. He was a big man and a loving father and occasionally he lifted Judith and swung her high up in the air. Judith was sombre, serious and shy and she always did as she was told. She did not pose any problems for the lady next door as far as child-minding was concerned.

Indeed, Judith preferred to be next door than to be home with her mother. Margaret would work at the milk bar from nine in the morning until six in the evening and then pick Judith up and take her home. As her mother turned the key and opened the door the child got herself ready to face the formidable silence. The silence and the airless smell. A deadness in the house. First Margaret would open the lounge-room window, then go to the kitchen and open the back door. The fresh air moved reluctantly through the house but never quite dispelled the staleness that lurked in the corners and the mustiness that hung about the walls. After the vitality and noise of the house next door, Judith did not know what to do with the silence. She would have liked to break it, to talk to her mother, to chatter and prattle and tell of her day but Margaret and silence were bound together. Judith did not know how to tear them apart.

Margaret would then run the bath and put Judith in it. She would go to the kitchen, cut up the potatoes, shell the peas, put the chops under the griller and then come back to wash Judith, swiftly and efficiently. She would leave Judith in the bath while she went to the kitchen to continue her cooking. When tea was almost ready she would get Judith out of the bath, dry her vigorously with a towel, put her pyjamas on, brush her hair and take her into the kitchen. They would sit at the kitchen table, one on each side, eating chops and peas and chips. After dinner, Judith would stay at the table while her mother washed the dishes. She knew she had to wait quietly and patiently until the last dish was dried and put away.

Then she could say, 'Give me a lolly.' Margaret would go to her bag and take out Judith's nightly treat. Would it be chocolate, a caramel, jubes, a lolly-pop? Judith never knew because Margaret brought something different home each night. Whatever it was, Judith would hold it and grasp it and love it. She would hug her arms around her mother's legs and whisper her thanks. If she held on too long, Margaret would disentangle her and tell her to go into the lounge-room. Judith would do as she was told and Margaret would follow with a bottle of beer, a glass, an ash-tray and a packet of cigarettes.

Margaret would turn on the radio and then sit in the deep lounge chair and pour herself a beer and light a cigarette. She would listen to popular songs and sometimes she would hum the melodies. Occasionally she would tune in to a radio play and she would listen in a haze of smoke. Judith would lie on the floor, colouring-in. At eight-thirty, Margaret would get up. 'Time for bed,' she'd say. 'Go to the toilet and clean your teeth.'

Judith would obey and, when she was in bed, her mother would come into the room, tuck her in and kiss her on the forehead. Sometimes Judith could not stop her arms from going up and winding themselves around her mother's neck. When that happened, her mother would untwine them and put them under the covers and tuck them in so tightly that, no matter how hard she tried, Judith could not get them out again. She went to sleep each night to the sounds of the radio playing in the lounge-room.

One night, about six months after Judith's fourth birthday, there was a knock at the door. Margaret went to see who it was and Judith followed her. When the door opened, Judith looked up and saw a monstrously ugly man. He was skinny and stooped and looked as if great handfuls of his face had been torn away.

'Yes, what do you want?' asked Margaret.

'It's me, Joe. I'm home,' the man said and fell crying into Margaret's arms. He cried and coughed and kept on coughing so that Margaret had to help him into the lounge-room and sit him in a chair and get him a glass of water.

'Shrapnel,' said Joe, after swallowing the water and when the coughing had eased. 'Tore the skin off my face. Damaged my chest and lungs. Lucky to be alive.' That was all Joe ever said about the war.

For the next two weeks he sat in a chair during the day with a rug around his knees, coughing, dozing, drinking sugared tea. He took very little notice of Judith. All his attention went into staying alive. Everything about him was rotting but he clawed onto life. He concentrated all day on finding fragments of energy, summoning them from the crevices of his crumbling body, stitching them together, hour by hour, so that, by night-time, he could thrust into his wife whatever vital force he had managed to weave together during the day. He would rut away at her, obsessed with his mission, until he had ejected his semen into her womb and then he would succumb to a fit of coughing that would leave him panting, breathless, lifeless. Margaret swallowed her revulsion. She tried to remember how she had loved him before he went to the war. She wiped his damp decaying body and covered him with warm blankets. He stank of death.

Judith could not sleep the night Joe came home. His torn face kept filling the space in front of her eyes and terror rose like vomit in her mouth. She wanted to rush to her mother, to hide in her skirts but she was put to bed early and the sheets pulled tight to imprison her. She heard them get into her mother's bed, heard murmurs and cries and moans and tears, heard the mournful creak of the bed springs, the sound of a rhythm she did not comprehend.

After that she would lie awake each night, waiting for it to begin, wondering what it was that she was hearing, wanting it to be over, dreading the gasping cough that marked its conclusion.

Margaret conceived quickly and when Joe realized that he had achieved what he set out to do, he gave up the nightly exercise and put all his energies into willing his body to remain alive until after the birth of his child. He would sit on the front verandah and very calmly breathe in the air. He would listen to the magpies and lift his face to the sun. He would drink egg-flips and sip beef tea and focus on getting well.

Now he took more notice of Judith and liked to have her with him. She would sit at his knee and put her head in his lap. He would place his hand gently on the top of her head, barely touching it, as if she were so fragile, so precious that a heavy touch might harm her. If she closed her eyes she could feel love flowing from his fingertips, infusing her and he could feel her heat, her life force, and he drew strength from her nearness. She grew used to his battered face and was aware only of the lips and eyes that smiled a warm welcoming.

'You must forgive your mother,' he would say, as they rested quietly together. 'The times have made her cold.' Judith did not understand what he was saying but she could feel the love behind the words.

The hollows of his body started to fill. Every day he grew stronger. Soon he was able to go for short walks and he took Judith with him. She learned to laugh and smile, to romp and play and she rejoiced in the respect that others showed her father. They did not seem to notice his scarred and ugly face. Judith now spent her days with him, instead of being looked after by the lady next door.

Meanwhile, Margaret ignored her pregnancy. She ignored Judith and she ignored Joe. The man who had returned to her was not the man who had gone away. Indeed, she felt him to be an intruder and, at times, wondered what he was doing in her house. She was astounded by his requests that she should give up working, smoking and alcohol in the interests of the unborn child. Life was a nightmare. The only way to make it bearable was to continue the pattern of existence that she had been following for the past four years. She worked at the milk bar; she came home and cooked the dinner; she sat in the lounge-room at night, listening to the radio, smoking and drinking beer.

'You must forgive your mother,' he would say again as he tucked Judith into bed and allowed the little arms to cling for as long as they needed to. He would nuzzle his face into his daughter's neck and rest his head there until he felt her hold relax, her breath deepen, her arms drop in sleep. And then he would look at her and choke with the wonder that a man could have fathered a child so exquisite. He wondered whether she would lose her beauty as she grew older or whether she would retain it and the wondering would pierce and stab and wound him because he knew that his mutilated lungs would not keep going long enough for him to know the answer.

Judith had turned five and begun school by the time her brother was born. Joe had been sure that another child would fix Margaret up, snap her into loving, awaken her maternal instincts. Joe's hopes remained unfulfilled. Margaret responded to the birth in the only way that made any sense to her. She again turned her face to the wall. She was no longer nineteen and she was no longer alone so this second rejection of a baby was inexcusable. Joe could not understand it and accused her of being cold, unfeeling, unnatural.

Margaret ignored everyone. She refused to see the baby, refused to feed it, refused to name it and if anyone talked about the baby at all she assumed a blankness that was impossible to penetrate.

Joe took them home but he was the one who had to look after his son. Margaret never heard the baby cry and behaved as if it did not exist. She went back to work at the milk bar as soon as possible.

Judith would rush home from school and watch her father tending the baby. She enjoyed seeing them together. She felt a fierce love for her brother and liked to hold him. Sometimes, however, when she held him, she was overcome by a strange compulsion to pinch his arm. Then he would cry and she would give him back to his father to be cuddled and kissed, petted and soothed. She never admitted to having been the cause of his distress.

When the baby was six months old he sat up for the first time. It was a Sunday and Margaret was at home. She was sitting outside in the garden reading the Sunday papers. Joe was so excited that he rushed out to her and told her that she must come and look at her clever son. Margaret went on reading. She didn't even look up. Joe grabbed the paper out of her hands, pulled her out of her chair and dragged her into the lounge-room.

'Look, damn you, look!' he shouted. She tried to turn her head away but Joe got behind her and held her head steady and made her look at the baby. Judith was sitting on the floor, next to her brother. She looked up to see her mother's mouth twisting against the pressure of her father's hand. When Margaret realized that she was trapped and could not move she closed her eyes to shut out the sight of her children. Then Joe started to beat her hard across the face, across the shoulders and across the back and all the time he was shouting, 'They're your children! Look at them! Look at them!'

Then he stopped hitting her. He let her go. She did not seem to know where she was for a moment. She sat on the floor, looking around her. She let her eyes rest on her children and, for the first time in a long time, Judith saw her mother smile.

'Mummy,' she murmured and crawled over to her mother and hugged her and felt, for the briefest moment, her mother's arms fold around her and press her close. Judith wanted the moment to last forever but Margaret let her go. Judith could see that her mother was still looking at the baby. Margaret got up and walked to the baby. She put out her arms and picked him up and held him tight. Then she walked out of the room carrying him.

Joe was crying with joy as he watched the mother hold his child. It seemed to him that all the disjointed pieces of his family's existence had suddenly slipped into their proper places. He picked Judith up and danced her about the room and they laughed and cried and tumbled and rolled all over the lounge-room floor.

All this play made him cough and he had to sit down while Judith brought him a glass of water. She patted his back and made him sip the water until his coughing eased. Trying to calm himself, he lay back in the chair, exhausted, his breathing rough and irregular.

Judith climbed up onto the lounge and looked out of the window into the backyard. The lawn sparkled green and bright flower beds gleamed with colour. She watched a bird flying about, swooping, curving upwards, diving, settling on the side fence. She could see her mother coming out of the garage, holding the baby in one arm and carrying a tin in the other. She marvelled at the sight of them together. She watched her mother walk to the centre of the green lawn. She sat down cross-legged with the baby secured in the space between her legs. She opened the tin and poured whatever was in the tin onto her clothes and onto the baby's clothes. Judith watched. Then she saw her mother take a box of matches out of her pocket and light one. In an instant, both she and the baby were ablaze. The baby gave one cry. Margaret remained silent. Judith stared. She tried to call her father but the scream was blocked in her throat. Finally she was able to let it out. She screamed a high, wailing cry. Joe jumped up and came to the window. He ran to the bedroom, grabbed a blanket and rushed outside.

He tried to smother them with the blanket but the petrol flames grew higher and higher until all three were engulfed, consumed and destroyed by Margaret's blinding need.

The only way that Judith's mind could deal with such a catastrophe was to blot it out. She repressed the fire altogether. She would not let herself remember her father or her mother or her brother. She lived as if the first six years of her life had not occurred.

She was put into a foster home where she was treated with meticulous care and attention. Her foster parents, who were not emotionally demonstrative people, never referred to her early childhood. They went along with the view that such things were better forgotten.

Judith started at a new school. She was quiet and withdrawn and devoted herself entirely to school work. She did not like to play, found it difficult to make friends with other children and preferred to lose herself in reading books. This legitimately removed her from the effort of engaging in normal childhood activities. Her escape from life into learning had a predictable result. She was always top of the class and although other children found her strange, they did not laugh at her. They treated her with respect and a slight feeling of awe.

Apart from her intellectual achievement, she had an unusual and daunting kind of beauty. Her skin was a warm honey-brown, her hair black and her eyes a vivid cat's eye green.

Adults stared at her. She was aware of the effect she had on them but she was also confused by it. She would often look at herself in the mirror to try to understand what it was about herself that fascinated others. As she grew older, she learned to like what she saw in the mirror and she came to accept the fact of her attractiveness. She felt secure and safe, spun within the threads of her own beauty.

By the time she was fifteen, most men who saw her either stared at her or followed her with their eyes as she passed by. She could feel her power but she saw it only as a force needed to sustain herself. Boys wanted to ask her out but were inhibited by the distance she constantly maintained. She had no wish to share herself with anyone. She needed all her beauty for herself.

She was, during these years, tortured at times by nightmares of blazing fires but she shook the dreams away. She had some recollection of a man who had held her once in a tight circle of love but she refused to pursue such memories. She lived on the surface of life and found study a suitable means of avoiding its depths. She was pleasant to others but had no close friends. She never participated in age-old discussions about the meaning of life or the nature of existence. Love and hate, happiness and sorrow, life and death were subjects she carefully avoided.

When she finished school she won a scholarship to Sydney University. Her foster parents had been kind but she had not allowed any real attachment to them to form and decided, at the age of eighteen, to leave them and live at a College while she studied at the University. Judith was committed to the concept of study but not to any particular course of study so she went to the University, during Orientation Week, to find out what courses were available.

She wandered around, bombarded by all that was exhibited, trying to take in all that was offered. She found herself strangely drawn to the School of Botany. She walked through the laboratories and looked at the specimens of dissected plants and was immediately enveloped by a sense of stillness.

The tranquil world of plants seemed much more attractive than the strident world of people and she found herself walking smartly through a small, paved, garden quadrangle to the Registrar's Office and asking for an enrolment form for the Faculty of Science. She filled it in swiftly, indicating on the form that she intended to major in Botany.

When Judith entered College and started her University course, no one knew her. She was, therefore, able to pursue her customary approach to life. She moved forward as if she had no past.

RHEUBEN

Rheuben's earliest memory was of his mother, Sophie, spooning chicken soup thick with noodles into his small mouth, crooning to him all the time, 'Come on, Rheuben, eat up your soup for Mama. Just another mouthful. How will you grow up to be a big strong boy if you don't eat up for your Mama?' while his father, Hymie, stood clapping his hands together, dancing in circles and singing a song in Yiddish to distract his son while his wife popped another spoonful into the infant mouth.

After the memory of the chicken soup there was the memory of the chopped chicken liver, the roast chicken, the potato cakes, the cheese blintzes that his mother constantly pressed upon him. Food was love, health, happiness. If only a boy would eat all his breakfast, lunch and dinner, his morning fruit, his afternoon cake and his hot milk and home-made biscuits for supper, all would be well.

Another early memory was sitting in the dark workroom behind his father's tailor's shop, listening to the hiss of the steam press, inhaling the harsh vapour that rose in intermittent bursts when his father pulled down the top of the press and used the foot pedal to force the steam through. When he took the trousers out they looked like shiny cardboard cutouts. Rheuben remembered running around the room trailing a giant horseshoe magnet, picking up all the pins that had fallen onto the workroom floor.

His mother, Sophie, minded the front of the shop. She knitted all day and sold the garments she made to the owner of a ladies' wear store. She would call Hymie from the workroom when a customer came in. Then Hymie would go to the front of the shop, his tape-measure around his neck, his thick spectacles half way down his nose, and, with his deft, pudgy hands, he would take a customer's measurements and write them down on a scrap of paper. He would help a customer choose the cloth and when he quoted the price of a suit, Rheuben could always hear his mother muttering under her breath, 'Hymie! What are you doing? You want to give the suit away?' Then Hymie would raise the price a little but never enough to satisfy his wife and she would turn her back on him and go into the workroom talking to herself and to her son.

'What's he running here? A charity, that's what. Not a business! The man has no head for business. How does he expect us to eat, eh, my little man? How does your father expect us to eat when he doesn't know how to charge for his work?' Rheuben found such comments confusing. His world was full to overflowing with things to eat. And she would pick Rheuben up and tweek his cheek vigorously and tell him, 'Not you, Rheuben. You won't grow up stupid like your father. No, my clever little man. A doctor! That's what my son will be, a doctor!' And she put him down and if he got bored he would take a piece of tailor's marking soap and draw patterns on the wooden floor.

By the time Rheuben started school he knew that there were two things he had to do. He had to eat up like a good boy and he had to be very clever. Being clever was no problem at all. In fact, Sophie and Hymie were somewhat in awe of his cleverness. He read early and loved solving mathematical problems and learning lists and dates. He was required to exhibit his prowess at family gatherings.

Rheuben's family was large and closely knit and he liked family get-togethers. He loved the splendour and luxury of their double-storied, Dover Heights homes. Uncle Abe owned a furniture factory. Uncle Max owned a ladies' clothing factory. Uncle Sam owned two large gift stores in the city. Uncle Abe's house had a games room with a full-sized billiard table and a table-tennis table for the children.

By comparison with the affluence of their relatives, Sophie and Hymie were poor. They lived in a small, dark flat in Bondi Road with worn lino on the kitchen floor and faded carpet in the poky lounge-room. The reason Hymie was poor, Sophie kept explaining, was that he was too generous. He was always selling suits at too low a price, always altering people's clothes for nothing, always giving money away to Jewish charities. He was Sophie's despair. She longed for a home like those of her sisters-in-law and her longing was all the more intense because she knew she would never have one. Her only consolation was that Rheuben was cleverer than all his cousins and that one day he would grow up to be a famous doctor. That would be her reward. To Sophie and Hymie, cleverness definitely took precedence over wealth.

When Rheuben was small he spent a lot of his time trying to avoid being touched. Sophie was always at him, bathing him, scrubbing his teeth, making sure his bottom was clean, brushing his hair, cleaning out his ears, drying between his toes, pulling him in and out of jumpers, buttoning up his coat, tying his shoelaces. She kept doing all these things long after the time when he should have been able to do them for himself. And then she would suddenly grab at him when he wasn't expecting it and hug him fiercely to her and press her lips onto his cheeks, smothering him with kisses. And Hymie wasn't much better. He could not keep his hands away from the curly head, could not walk along with his son without putting an arm around his shoulder, could not have gone to sleep at night without going into Rheuben's room for a last look, a last touch, a last kiss on the forehead. Rheuben was touched so often that he never wanted to touch, kissed so often that he never wanted to kiss, hugged so often that he never felt the need to hug anyone back. He often felt that he might drown in the eiderdown of feathers that covered him at night.

Above all, he feared that his Nanny might tickle him to death. She was large and thick and foreign and whenever he saw her, which was at least once a week, he had to kiss her 'Hello' and kiss her 'Goodbye'. The apprehension would begin as they approached the red-bricked, triple-fronted, wide-windowed, Dover Heights bungalow her sons had built for her. As the doorbell rang, his apprehension changed to fear. He could hear her moving heavily down the hall. Fear turned to terror as she opened up the door.

'Ah! Mine beautiful boy!' she would exclaim with ecstasy and crush him in a two-armed grip that forced the breath to rush out of his lungs. He wondered if he would ever be able to breathe in again. Then she would carry him into the lounge-room and lower herself into a straight-backed chair and, without releasing him, she would stand him between her legs. She would let go her grip with her right arm but keep him clamped in place with her left arm and then she would begin to tickle him. She would tickle him under the chin, under the arm, under the ribs, chortling and laughing in her heavy Polish accent. It was difficult, under the circumstances, to smile or laugh but he had to make himself do so. He knew that she would not let him go until she heard what she considered to be a genuine sign of joy.

Then she would let him go and he would sit down in an armchair, recovering, while his father and his grandmother talked away in Polish. He did not understand anything they said but he did not mind. He was grateful to have their attention turned elsewhere. After half an hour, his grandmother would tell him to go into the kitchen to have something to eat. The kitchen was dim and quiet. He would turn on the light and sit at the nook at the back of the kitchen. On the table there would be a plate of neck-ties, sweet thin strips of pastry shaped like knotted ties and dusted with castor sugar. There would be six neck-ties on the plate and a large glass of milk beside them. Rheuben would eat them all, as slowly as possible, and sip the milk. He took his time, partly because it was a lot for a little boy to eat and he knew Nanny would be upset if he did not eat all she had set out for him, and partly because he wanted to postpone the moment when he would have to go back to the lounge-room and face the ordeal of being kissed 'Goodbye.'

When Rheuben started school he was given a violin and taught to play it. When he was seven he was recognized as a child prodigy. He had to practise his violin for one and a quarter hours every day. Uncle Abe recognized genius when he saw it and he paid for the music lessons. He also paid for a member of the Sydney Symphony Orchestra to listen to the child practise and he paid a man to pick Rheben up from home and drive him to school so that he could spend more time at his violin. He started performing at concerts when he was eight and the whole family, not just Hymie and Sophie, relied on him to become a concert violinist when he grew up, in addition, of course, to becoming a famous doctor.

He was the pet, the wonder, the loved one; a constant centre of attention to be touched, admired, hugged, kissed; to be questioned and tested on general knowledge; to be listened to in absolute silence when he played his violin at weekly family gatherings.

Rheuben would have liked to have fulfilled all his family's ambitions for him but the main thing that concerned him about playing the violin was that the long hours of standing up made his feet and legs so tired. His calf muscles ached and he longed for practice time to be over just so he could sit down. He practised with precision but slowly the heart went out of his playing.

When he was eleven, his teacher at the Conservatorium of Music asked him if he really liked playing the violin. No one had ever asked him that before. The question came as a shock but it did not take him long to find the true answer.

'I don't like it at all,' he replied. The teacher told Sophie that, although Rheuben played skillfully, he did not have the soul of a musician and she should give up any ideas of him becoming a concert violinist. Rheuben remembered walking out of the Conservatorium with a sense of elation. He felt that he had been set free and that he would never have to practise again. However, his family would not give up so easily. They found him a different teacher.

During Rheuben's early childhood, then, two things were of great importance – the violin and the world of the Jews. The whole of his week was organized to keep him securely folded within the arms of Judaism. First of all, there had been the matter of choosing the correct school. Families like theirs, from all over the Easter suburbs, sent their children to Bellevue Hill Public School, so that's where Rheuben went. His friends were his cousins and other Jewish children he had known since birth. He was clever and therefore it was assumed that he would go to Woollahra Opportunity School. He did so when he was eleven. After his first day at the new school the only thing Hymie wanted to know was how many Jewish children were in his class. Out of a class of thirty, twelve were Jews.

Although he learned about Blaxland, Lawson and Wentworth, Bourke and Wills and the Eureka Stockade, Australian history meant nothing. The only relevance lay in being Jewish and being lucky to be alive. 'If our parents hadn't left Poland before World War II, then you wouldn't be alive today,' Hymie would tell him, over and over again. 'The only way we Jews can survive is to stick together.'

For as long as he could remember, Rheuben had gone to synagogue with Hymie every Saturday morning. They would catch the bus to the end of Oxford Street and then walk through Hyde Park to the Great Synagogue in Elizabeth Street. Riding on the sabbath was forbidden and Hymie didn't want the Rabbi to think he had caught the bus. That's why they had to walk the last few blocks to the synagogue.

He would sit next to Hymie with a skull cap on his head and a small prayer shawl around his neck. His cap was white satin with a candelabrum embroidered in gold thread and blue thread around the edges. His mother usually came in later and sat upstairs with the women. She whispered to her friends when no one was looking. After sitting with his father for about an hour he would join the other children, boys and girls, in a room at the back of the synagogue where a children's service was conducted. The boys took part in the service and learned what it was all about. The girls were only allowed to join in the choruses. He liked the songs and sang in a high, pure voice.

Every Sunday morning he attended Sunday School in class-rooms at the Bondi Junction Synagogue and two afternoons a week he walked from his school to the synagogue for Hebrew lessons. By the time he was twelve he knew a lot about being a Jew. He knew why he had to eat kosher food, he knew about Passover and Succoth and the Day of Atonement. He knew all about the suffering and the centuries of decimation. He had a pretty good idea by now why so many Jews seemed to be clever. All the dumb ones had been eliminated over hundreds of years of persecution.

When he turned twelve he had to prepare for his Bar Mitzvah and this meant private lessons with the Cantor two afternoons a week.

For recreation he belonged to the Great Synagogue Youth and every Sunday attended a stamp group, or a debate, or a film night or went on some outing with other Jewish children his own age. In the holidays there were picnics and hikes and camps.

By the time he did all this, practiced his violin and attended weekly family gatherings there was not much time left. However they did mange to find a few spare hours to have him taught tennis, horse-riding, ice-skating and swimming. Uncle Abe paid for the lessons. It was thought necessary for a Jewish child to have all these accomplishments if he was going to adapt himself successfully to life in Australia.

When he turned thirteen, he was, according to Jewish law, a man. He did not feel like one. On the day of his Bar Mitzvah, he sang his portion of the service efficiently and the family were well satisfied. He wore a new grey flannel suit with long trousers and that, as much as his performance in the synagogue, marked his entry into the world of men. They had a big reception for him at the Maccabean Hall and he had to make a speech and everyone was proud of him.

He received six fountain pens, four leather writing cases, three paper-weights and four sets of silver-backed brush and comb sets as well as a lot of books and a great deal of money. It was a bewildering experience as he had not yet reached puberty and the idea of being a man was frightening. There were, however, some positive aspects to being a man. His mother stopped brushing his hair and no longer looked to see if he had washed behind his ears. His grandmother stopped tickling him and the family, in general, allowed him to exist without putting upon him either an overflow of physical affection or a demand to display his intelligence.

Hymie took Rheuben into his room and told him it was now time for him to learn the facts of life. Rheuben went red in the face and hung his head, unwilling to admit that he and his friends already knew all that they needed to know. Hymie made him sit on the floor while he read painstakingly to his son from the Golden Pathway book of sex education for boys. Hymie read every word on every page and when he came to an illustration he pushed the book under Rheuben's eyes saying, 'Look!'

At the end of the reading Hymie closed the book and, looking up at the ceiling, told Rheuben that Jewish boys were good boys. They did not do that sort of thing until they were married. Then he got up, rubbed his hands together, sighed with satisfaction and walked out of the room.

One day, when Rheuben was fourteen, he was lying on his stomach on Bondi Beach. His head faced the water and he looked up to see a large-bosomed woman emerging from the sea. Her breasts swung in her scant bikini top and he felt his penis stiffen as he watched her walk up the beach. In a few moments he felt a mighty explosion that he thought had torn him apart. He looked around and was surprised that no one had noticed the momentous thing that had happened to him. He went into the surf to wash away the sticky wetness.

He was growing tall and handsome and would soon have to shave. Girls liked him and he danced cheek to cheek with them at the Great Synagogue Youth Dances. Often the lights were dimmed and he would kiss whoever he was dancing with but at eleven o'clock all the fathers would turn up to drive their children home. They were as protective of their sons as they were of their daughters.

He enjoyed the fact that girls liked him but most of his time was devoted to study, to the violin, to being captain of the school debating team. His life was so full of things that he had to do that he never had time to consider what life might be about.

When Rheuben was seventeen, he decided to give up playing the violin. He told his parents that he could no longer spare the time for practicing. He was in his final year of high school. If they wanted him to do well at his studies then he would have to give up his music. Hymie agreed immediately. Sophie cried for a week but had to acquiesce. This decision, and his parents' acceptance of it, marked his first gesture of independence.

In the Christmas holidays after he had finished school, when he had just turned eighteen, he met a girl called Simone on Bondi Beach. She was Jewish but had been born in France and had recently migrated to Australia with her mother. She was twenty-four years old. She was small and blonde, with large teeth and a wide smile. Within a week she had won him to the point where he declared his eternal love and wanted to live with her forever. They spent their days in his bedroom and she initiated him into the rites of manhood while Sophie and Hymie were hard at work in the tailor's shop.

He introduced her proudly to his parents and was surprised by the coldness with which they received her. Polish Jews did not trust French Jews and, besides, the girl was much too old for their Rheuben. He took her into his room at night and put the record player on while he made love to her.

'What are they doing in there, Hymie?' Sophie would ask worriedly.

'They're listening to records,' Hymie would reply, shrugging his shoulders, trying to hide from her the deepness of his concern.

Simone decided quite quickly that she and Rheuben should get married and Rheuben, besotted as he was with his first love, could think of nothing he wanted more. He told his parents what he wanted to do. Simone could work and he could still go to university.

Hymie took him aside. 'I'm an old man,' he said. 'I'm not clever like you but this I'll tell you. The girl doesn't love you. She's looking for a husband. You're eighteen years old. Just a boy. You don't know nothing about these things. Believe your father. Ask her to wait for two years. Tell her you'll marry her in two years' time. Find out for yourself.'

Rheuben was so sure that Simone loved him that he was not afraid to put her to the test. He was shocked to find her declaring that they would have to marry now or not at all. She left him without a tear and Hymie was proven to be right. Rheuben thought he might die of a broken heart but found he was still alive when the University year began. Before he went to enrol, he performed a second, and most important gesture of independence. He informed his parents that they would have to give up their dream of him becoming a doctor. He felt that his talents best lay in the Law. He intended to take an Arts-Law degree and become a barrister. Hymie and Sophie took the news better than he had expected them to. Sophie found it relatively easy to move from her fantasy of 'My son, the doctor,' to 'My son, the barrister.'

When he began university he realized how narrow and enclosed his life had been. He sat in on the Humanist society, the Libertarian Society and meetings of various political groups. He drank coffee in Manning House and the Union, went to the pub for a beer. He met students who were studying English and Philosophy, Government and Anthropology, Architecture and Science. Girls were drawn to his sensuality. He learned very quickly how to attract, win, bed them. The structure of his early upbringing tumbled away and he considered himself to be very liberated in thought and deed.

He now found his parents something of an embarrassment. He would look at them and marvel at the fact that he had come from them. They were small and round and foreign and he was tall and handsome and lean. They were dull and homely and locked into their heritage. He felt that he had broken free. He did not bring friends home. He did not want his newly made acquaintances to see his origins.

He persuaded his parents to allow him to live in a College. He would be closer to the University and would benefit by living in a studious atmosphere. He had a scholarship and a living allowance and, by working as a waiter two nights a week, was able to earn his pocket-money. He always visited his parents on Friday nights.

In College he met boys who came from large properties in the country and wealthy city boys whose parents preferred them to live-in. Such boys had what Rheuben came to see as breeding and breeding was something that Rheuben wished to acquire.

He made a great effort to learn from them. He learned to ask politely for the butter or the salt to be passed to him, instead of leaning across the table to get it for himself. He learned not to put his elbows on the table during a meal. He learned that white wine goes with fish and red with meat. Such niceties were of no significance to the Jews.

He spent long nights with fellow college students discussing morality, sex, religion, marriage. He was eager to absorb a cultural heritage other than his own.

His aims were now quite clear. He wanted to do very well in his studies and he wanted to cultivate the attributes of good taste and breeding. If he could do that then he would be able to drag himself out of the suffocating insularity of his origins. His parents were to have no further influence on his life. He intended to move into the future by means of denying the past.

RHEUBEN AND JUDITH

They did not meet immediately. In fact, Rheuben had been attending university for two years before Judith arrived. He was about to begin the final year of his Arts degree. He was undertaking distinction work in Political Science and Philosophy. Both subjects excited him and he felt some regret that he would soon have to give up student life and enter the hard world of Law School. His career was clearly planned. He had obtained a position as an Articled Clerk with a solid, well-known firm of Sydney solicitors. He would start work with them in a year's time and would stay with them during his four-year law course. This would give him the necessary experience and contacts to enable him to become a barrister at the end of his studies and the pay, although small, would be enough for him to support himself. Meanwhile, he was delighted to have this last year in which he could pursue his interests and enjoy himself.

He felt very confident in his relationships with women. He had learned a good lesson from his first love affair. His attitude to women was now quite sensible and tailored to suit his career intentions. He made it clear to any potential girlfriend that he would not allow himself to fall in love and that he would not commit himself seriously to any woman until he had established himself as a barrister. He ended a relationship whenever he felt that a woman wanted more than he was prepared to give and he never had any difficulty in acquiring a new girlfriend.

He had become a well-known figure on the campus. He was highly regarded for his clever and witty debating style and represented the university in inter-state debating competitions.

He wrote articles for '*Honi Soit*', the university newspaper, and was an active member of the Students' Representative Council. He had an abundance of vitality and warmth.

On the day Judith first came to the university, he was sitting at a table in Science road, chatting to new students and handing out pamphlets on Student Council activities. He was flirting with two blonde, long-haired Arts students when Judith climbed to the top of the stone staircase and set foot on Science Road. As she stood at the top of the steps, hesitant and unfamiliar, he caught sight of her and, in an instant, her face and form flooded his eyes, his head, his hands, his mouth until he was filled brimful with her presence.

He could not speak. He could not move. So shocked was he that he could not breathe. He believed in logic and rational thought, yet here he was, faced with the inexplicable. He believed absolutely in the conscious control of life, yet here he was, struck down by fate. For he saw her immediately in this way, as if she had been sent to him, as if she were someone he had been waiting for, as if she were something which he must, necessarily, acquire. He felt all his certainties and assurances crumble around him. He knew if he could not have her, own her, possess her, love her, marry her, then his life would be meaningless. A moment before he had held his destiny tightly secured in the palm of his hand. Now he was stunned and disordered.

As he looked at her he extended his range of vision to take in the effect she had on others. He observed that men and women alike stared at her, for Judith carried her beauty with such assurance and such nobility that she compelled all who saw her to look again, out of envy or admiration or desire.

He watched the way men students went up to her, asked if they could help her, tried to flirt with her. She smiled cool dismissals and went on her way. She approached each table, collected pamphlets, looked at them, put them in her bag.

As she approached Rheuben's table, he pulled himself together and began laughing and flirting with the two long-haired Arts students. Judith stopped at the table. She fingered the pamphlets. Rheuben made himself continue his conversation. He put his arm around one of the girls and, smiling warmly, asked her if she would go out with him that night. When she agreed, he turned to Judith, his arm still around the girl, and told her to help herself to anything on the table that interested her. Her eyes caught his in a snap of icy green as she picked up a few pamphlets and walked away.

He decided that he must approach the matter of winning Judith in a calm and logical way. He wanted to fling himself at her feet, to declare his love and longing, to beg for mercy, to plead for a sign that there might be some hope for him. But he could see that she would simply brush him away.

He set himself to studying her habits and finding out as much as he could about her. He knew many university people and he soon learned who she was, where she lived, what course she was studying. He found out her lecture timetable and would appear, at odd times, in places where he knew she would be. He made sure he was always with friends and he never gave the impression of noticing her.

And his method worked because she did notice him. She would see him in Manning House, sitting with his friends, laughing and talking while she sat alone, drinking coffee during the afternoon break between lectures. She was attracted by his exuberance, his vitality, his warmth, for she was empty and lacked the qualities that he possessed.

A great many male students had asked her to go out with them but she was afraid and refused and devoted herself totally to her studies. She took no notice of the men who did approach her but she noticed Rheuben because he did not approach her at all.

When Rheuben decided that it was time to act he was astounded at the ease with which he won her. He approached her table and asked if he might sit with her to drink his coffee. She smiled a tentative agreement. He began to talk to her of himself, his life at university, his joy in being there, his love of people, his attachment to friends. He told her that he had noticed her, had felt she was too much alone, that she was missing out on much that university had to offer and asked her if she would like to come that night to listen to him in a university debate.

She came and when he saw her sitting in the hall he was spurred on to a brilliance of speech and an excellence of delivery that won him the high praise of the adjudicator and the hearty applause of the audience. Afterwards, he went to her and introduced her to his friends and took her with them to drink coffee and talk and although she did not have much to say, he could see that he had won her admiration and respect. He involved her in other student activities. He took her to talks and meetings, to university films and plays but always with a group of friends. She enjoyed listening to intellectual discourse, analysis of films, exposition of literature, political arguments. She did not contribute but the listening brought a light to her eyes and a smile to her lips.

Rheuben and his friends would spend many hours arguing philosophy at the entrance to Fisher library, sitting in the stone archways surrounding the large quadrangle. Judith knew where to find them and would often come there at dusk to watch the last rays of the afternoon sun slanting through the stone towers and to listen to discussions which seemed able to solve the problems of the world.

She found, through Rheuben, something she had never known before – acceptance and friendship. Rheuben's friends took their cue from him. They pretended to ignore her beauty and yet felt privileged that she, so desired by others, so aloof from others, chose to spend her time with them. They tried to draw her out, questioned her about her course, encouraged her to express her thoughts and ideas, but she would smile and look away and they were not put off by her refusal, for the aesthetic pleasure of her presence outweighed all other considerations.

Gradually he began to single her out, to engineer walking with her alone, to ask her to accompany him on outings outside the university grounds. She felt so secure in their friendship that she did not hesitate in accepting. She liked to be with him. He always made her laugh and smile. When she was attending lectures or studying or alone in her room, she did not feel alive. At such times she often felt coldness and emptiness, darkness and death. When she was with Rheuben, his vitality filled up her hollow spaces and she took on the reflected glow of his life force.

When he sensed that the time was right he told her of his love and it seemed to Judith that the words he murmured were an echo of her own inner thoughts and the love he spoke found a mirror in her eyes.

He held her gently then and said their love was forever and she felt a great sigh well up inside her and tears began to fall and he licked the tears with his tongue and pressed his lips to her eyelids but the tears kept falling and her shoulders started heaving and great, shuddering sobs shook her body and he did not understand but he held her and soothed her and calmed her. And he wanted to know why she had cried like that but she could not answer him. She only knew that she felt happy and relieved, safe and secure, so she told him that and he was satisfied and they walked along with their arms around each other in the sure knowledge that they were going to live happily ever after.

He took her then to his room and locked the door. He led her to the bed and lay down beside her – caressing, touching, soothing, murmuring. He let his eyes feed on her face, feature by feature, trying to understand the nature of her beauty. Strong square jaw, wide sensuous mouth, lips drawn back in a faint smile from large, even, white teeth, high cheekbones, almond eyes, green now flecked with amber sparks, high brow, heavy dark hair, a slight dimple in the left cheek. It was not any particular aspect that was beautiful but rather the arrangement of the features, the very structure of the face that gave it such a unique quality, and the power she had to stun and shock came from the extraordinary colour combinations – the green eyes, white teeth, pink lips sprang in violent contrast from the rich gold-brown skin.

He took off his clothes and then began to undress her, slowly, gently. She did not resist him. And when she was naked he gazed at her and took in her wholeness and he knew that nothing would ever surpass this first sight of her. His breath caught sharply and he trembled with the wonder that this prize was his. He examined her minutely from head to toe. His fingers traced her shape. He let his palm, fingers spread, run slowly down her body, traversed her thighs with the soft pads of finger tips. Her skin was warm and dry and velvet to his touch and he let his lips brush the smooth skin on the insides of her thighs. The softness here made him dizzy with desire and he had to rest his head in the hollow of her belly. He breathed in her scent with long, deep breaths and he felt he might drown in his ecstasy. He lifted his hands to caress the curving breasts, firm, honey-brown, soft-tipped. He drew himself further up, kissing and touching her face, her neck, her eyes, her hair. She lay passively, smiling lightly, eyes closed, accepting his adoration. He knew it was her first time and he entered her gently. She winced slightly but did not resist his entry and once he was inside her he could not hold back.

When he was finished he apologised to her, told her that he had been too excited, that it would be better next time, that he would teach her how to enjoy her body. She did not answer but clung fiercely to him and did not want to let him go.

It was not any better the next time, or the time after that. In fact, it was not ever any better. She never resisted him. She wanted him to hold her, to touch her, to kiss her, to undress her, to make love to her but her body did not respond. His sexual affairs had been numerous and he knew that he was a good lover. He felt that he would eventually find a way to evoke a sexual response in Judith and bring her to orgasm. He tried to talk to her about the matter but she did not want to listen.

He came to realize that what she wanted was his adoration. She was his goddess and she needed him to worship her and bring his sexuality to her as a humble offering. She longed for the constant renewal of his wonder and awe at the sight of her nakedness. And, indeed, he was able to fulfil her requirements. Her body obsessed his waking thoughts and he lived to lose himself again in the spell of her flesh.

She needed more than this. She needed constant words, assurances and reassurances. She never tired of his telling her how he had longed for her from the moment he had set eyes on her, how he had watched her that first day, how he had pretended to be interested in other girls to make her jealous, how he had followed her, set himself in her path, observed her while pretending to ignore her, how he had plotted to win her, how he had known from the first instant that he would love her forever and not just forever but forever and a day and not just forever and a day but for all eternity. He would speak these words as he caressed her and she would float on the waves of his words, float far away on a tide of ecstasy that he witnessed but could not share, observed but could not reach. Then he would long to bring her back to himself, to here, to now, to his flesh, to his penis, to his love. In a frenzy he would enter her but no matter how violently he thrust himself into her, he could not penetrate her world. She would not come back to him and he would empty himself into her with a sense of bitterness and defeat. Then he would stop and move away and she would open her eyes, hurt and bewildered, and beg him to lie beside her once again. She would hold him and press her breasts against him and wind her legs about him and run her hands through his hair and tell him that she loved him forever and for all eternity. In this way she seemed to turn his defeat into victory.

They walked through the university grounds, arm in arm, and this gave Rheuben the opportunity to exhibit his triumph to all. How they must envy him, to carry on his arm a woman of such unparalleled beauty! Judith felt no less pride because Rheuben's intelligence, vitality and charm made him a fitting mate. They were dazzled by their own perfection. Prince and Princess. Darlings of the gods. Their lives shimmered in sunlight, their days swirled in joy.

They were determined that, hand in hand, they could achieve whatever they set out to do. A combination of intelligence, good looks and unqualified determination would enable them to acquire all the good things in life.

They planned their life accordingly. They would marry at the end of the year, pool their resources and move into a small flat close to the university. Judith would complete her degree and then work for four years. By this time Rheuben would have finished his law degree and had two years to establish himself as a barrister. By then they should be able to buy a house and start a family. Perfect.

They married at the Registry Office and the only witnesses were their friends. Judith saw no reason to invite her foster parents and Rheuben certainly had no intention of telling Hymie and Sophie about his marriage until it was an accomplished fact. Judith was nineteen years old. Rheuben was twenty-one. He hired a dress suit with tails and a top hat and she bought a long, clinging, low-cut, white satin gown. Her veil was long and she carried white lilies. They made a stunning sight, enjoying a picnic with their friends in Hyde Park after the ceremony.

He took her to meet his parents and introduced her as his wife. Sophie burst into tears and Hymie wrung his hands in despair. 'Beautiful, yes, but not Jewish!' he murmured to Rheuben in a quiet aside. Rheuben felt so far removed from his origins that his parents' distress did not touch him. He laughed at them and called them old-fashioned and told them that the world would be a better place if there were no religions at all.

Hymie sighed and told Rheuben he was a fool. 'You should have married your own kind,' he warned. 'One day you'll see I'm right.' Rheuben smiled smugly, kissed his mother goodbye, patted his father's shoulder and swept his bride away.

He began to work in the solicitor's office and to attend lectures at the Law School. He worked hard at his studies and at cultivating the right kind of friends. The prestigious law firm he worked for soon recognized his superior talents and paid him more than they would normally pay an articled clerk. Judith no longer mixed with people at the university. She attended lectures, worked part-time as a tutor in the Botany Department, studied and spent the rest of the time being Rheuben's wife, learning to cook well for select dinner parties, acquiring a taste for antique furniture, budgeting carefully so that money could be accumulated to buy Noritake dinnerware, Orefors wine glasses, Sheffield silver-plate cutlery, chrystal bowls, Lalique ashtrays and fine linen table cloths.

She became the perfect hostess – decorative, reserved, charming as she served unusual but perfect meals to her guests. And Rheuben provided the zest, exuberance, the fine wine, the stimulating conversation. No one ever refused an invitation to dinner.

Everything went according to plan. Judith completed her degree and took a full-time job as a Research Assistant in the Botany Department. The job was not well paid but suited her interests and needs. Rheuben did splendidly. On graduation he set up as a barrister and his firm of solicitors gave him a large number of their Workers' Compensation cases. He quickly established himself as a sound barrister with impeccable courtroom style. By the end of a year he was making a great deal of money. By the end of the second year they were able to buy a house.

They chose a modern Pettit and Sevitt home in St. Ives with a bewitching bush setting, skylight windows, exposed beam ceilings and an open country-style kitchen. Long-haired, white carpet featured in the lounge-room, offset by a black leather lounge suite. Smart black and white striped curtains hung at either side of the picture window. The dining-room table was a charming oval antique with high-backed chairs upholstered in deep purple velvet and a well-matched antique sideboard against one wall. All the walls and ceilings in the house were white.

An open wooden staircase spiralled upstairs into the family room which was suitably carpeted in a functional, low-pile, tweedy-brown. Off the family room ran the master-bedroom with its whiteboard bed, turquoise satin coverlet, walk-in wardrobe and en-suite bathroom featuring white bath and toilet with a white and rust-brown tiled floor. Large, thick, rust-coloured towels hung on wide towel racks against the white walls. A main bathroom and two other small bedrooms also branched off the family room – accommodation for the two children who would eventually occupy them.

Judith was twenty-five and Rheuben twenty-seven when they reached this summit and they reached it by paying no attention to all the tangled undergrowth, the thorny bushes and the gnarled trees that they had trampled down in order to make their ascent possible. They stood on the top and all they could see was the clear, panoramic vision of the splendid life that lay before them.

If they had been courageous enough to turn their heads, if they had faced the life that lay behind them, if they had sifted through and sorted out their scattered debris, then they might have been able to avert their tragedy.

But neither of them ever looked back and, as a consequence, they were soon to be enmeshed in darkness and despair.

RHEUBEN

Rheuben was not happy but he did his utmost to hide this fact from himself and he certainly managed to hide it from everyone else.

His chambers in Phillip Street were richly comforting. He arrived there at seven o'clock each weekday morning. He told himself, and everyone else, that he liked an early start and that, by leaving St. Ives at quarter past six, he avoided the heavy traffic.

He liked the morning drive in his comfortable, air-conditioned Volvo. He played his favourite classical music on cassettes on his way to town – Dvojak or Vivaldi or Sibelius. From the moment he started his car and put on his music he could forget Judith and the house at St. Ives and he could begin to enjoy his day.

He had a permanent parking spot in the Domain Car Park and it was only a ten minute walk from there to his chambers. He liked the brisk, cool air of the empty city streets, the sight of the leafy trees and the sound of the pigeons in Hyde Park. He invariably shivered as he crossed Queen Victoria Square and turned right into Phillip Street. The winds here were always cold, even on a summer's day. He could never suppress the smile that came to his lips as he entered the building that housed his chambers. The smile expressed his satisfaction in owning rooms in this prestigious building. He took the lift to the ninth floor and emerged to breathe in the silence of his plush surroundings. Down the hall, past the unoccupied floor secretary's desk, along the thick, chocolate-brown carpet to room 907. Insert the key. Enter. The large mahogany desk glowing in the semi-darkness. Turn on the light. The room a tasteful blend of light and dark. Cream, self-embossed, striped wall paper, deep shelves lined with heavy, leather-bound law books, carefully chosen light-coloured abstracts, brown velvet drapes. The splendid leather armchair behind the desk held the imprint of Rheuben's body and it seemed to beckon him to slip into the familiar, welcoming shape.

Here he would sit and lose himself in work, preparing opinions or working on a court case until his secretary brought him the mail and a cup of fresh, percolated coffee at nine o'clock. From then on his day would vary. He might have appointments with clients; he might have to appear in court; he might have to immerse himself in paper work all day. He was never bored. His work absorbed him totally but the thing he enjoyed most was to appear in court. He liked to don his wig and winged collar and black gown and saunter to the courts. The challenge of a court appearance stimulated him; the need to prove a case taxed his wits and sharpened his mode of delivery. It was a theatre in which he must act a new role each day, a stage on which he must be alert enough to change his performance at a moment's notice. He was so competent that a decision seldom went against him, with the result that he was never short of clients. He specialized in workers' compensation cases and was rapidly becoming an expert in medical aspects of the law. He worked a six-day week, from seven in the morning until six in the evening, although he made sure that he took time off to lunch with influential acquaintances and friends.

Rheben's life at work, then, was both demanding and rewarding and, if Rheuben was not happy, then it is quite certain that his unhappiness was in no way connected with his work.

When Rheuben left his chambers at six o'clock in the evening, turned off the lights and locked the door, walked back along the corridor and past the empty floor secretary's desk, into the lift and down to the ground floor, along Phillip Street and across windswept Queen Victoria Square, past the dark park and down into the empty hollows of the car park, he would pull his coat collar firmly around his neck in an effort to ward off the inner chill that would now begin to come upon him. A deep melancholy suffused him and he would try to shake it off. He would get into his car and drive out of the car park trying to be cheerful, smiling goodnight to the attendant at the exit, easing the car into the line of traffic that was making its way onto the Harbour Bridge. Some music might help but he often found himself putting on Beethoven and Bach and that meant that his melancholy might well give way to despair.

Sometimes he found himself heading for Bondi instead of St. Ives and he might be half way to his parents' place before he realized what he was doing. He would go inside the small, warm, steamy flat and sit with his parents for a while. Sophie would try to tempt him with food while Hymie circled him, rubbing his hands together, grinning, murmuring, 'Well, well, well.' They would ask no questions but would wait and listen while Rheuben told them about his work, a recent case he had won, an interesting person he had met. They devoured his words, swallowed them whole without digesting them, for the truth of the matter was that they were so joyful at seeing Rheuben that they could not look at him and listen to him at one and the same time.

He did not quite know why he came to see them but what he needed was to witness the closeness of their union. He felt their oneness the moment he entered their home and, in the same instant, he felt his own alienation from them. He kept returning because he needed to renew the knowledge that these two pudgy, foreign people loved each other, understood each other, knew each other in a way that he and Judith did not know each other and did not love each other and did not understand each other. He came to find out their secret. Hymie and Sophie would have given Rheuben anything. They would have given him their very lives but they did not know what he came for so they could not give him the thing he sought. He always left them empty-handed.

They would beg him, next time (may God forgive him his sin), to bring his wife to visit them. Though he had broken their hearts, though he had committed an unforgivable crime, though he had abandoned God and the Jewish people, though he had cast aside five thousand years of sacred tradition, though his wife was a shiksa and his children would be goyem, though he had done all this . . . he was their Rheuben, their son, their love, the light of their life, their reason for living. Please, next time, he should be good enough to bring his wife. Not to a big family gathering; that, of course, was impossible, but just to the privacy of his parents' home. What harm could there be in that? The uncles and aunts would never know. Perhaps God himself, in his mercy, would be gracious enough to close his eyes.

Rheuben would have to shut his heart against the deluge of their words for, had he listened, he might easily have been overwhelmed. So he would leave them with a sigh, a kiss, a soft pressure of warm hands and drive away home to Judith and St. Ives.

As he drove home he would feel depression gathering at his temples, spreading across the back of his head, travelling down his neck and settling, with determination, on his shoulders. There it would sit and there it would stay until he left the house the next morning. Yet he tried to fight it, refused to submit to it, was determined to find a way to eliminate it.

He would invariably enter the house cheerfully, calling out to Judith to announce his arrival, apologizing for being late, asking her about her day. The first sight of her, even after six years of marriage, still had the power to shock him. He would feel, always, a momentary catch of breath, a sudden contracting spasm in the stomach, a flash of wonder at the precious quality of her beauty. She would always hesitate and stand still for this moment of adoration, like an actress in a spotlight waiting for applause. When the moment was over, she would go to him to be kissed. Sometimes he wanted to ask her why she never kissed him first, why she always gave him her cheek to be kissed but he knew that if he asked her such a thing she would merely look at him, startled and surprised, without in any way understanding the point of the question.

The trouble was that if Rheuben tried to discuss any of his dissatisfaction with their relationship, Judith always looked so puzzled and confused that he was unable to accuse her of dissatisfying him when she did everything she could to serve him. Although she worked full-time, she did all the housework herself, looked after the garden, cooked him magnificent meals, kept his clothes immaculate, was amenable to accompanying him on all social occasions, was happy to provide elegant dinner parties and never complained about his long working hours.

These were actions of love, gestures of love, proof of love and yet they did not add up to love. Rheuben felt unloved. His worship of Judith, his adoration of her body had failed to awaken any sexual response in her. She always allowed him to make love to her but the quality of their love-making had not changed. Their sexual exchanges still consisted of his adoration and her acceptance of his adoration. She was still the goddess and he the slave. The more he loved her the more tormented he became by his failure to bring her to orgasm. He, so full of longing, so vulnerable, envied her blissful, unassailable, impenetrable state of mind. And yet he could not accuse her of neglect for she sought to anticipate and to fulfil all his material needs.

He did not know what to do. He wanted to crack open what he believed to be her enigmatic nature but she had a way of stopping any conversation that might involve looking inside herself for an answer. She would only talk on the level of what she had done at work that day or what he had done or what books she had read or what she should cook at the next dinner party. He did not know how to penetrate her armour but he continued to believe that one day he would find a way. He felt, at times, that he should make love to other women in order to assure himself that he was capable of bringing a woman to sexual satisfaction. He wanted to be certain that the fault lay with Judith and not with himself. Opportunities arose from time to time but when it came to the point he could not be unfaithful to her. Her body continued to obsess his sexual thoughts and he devoted the hours he was with her to showering her with love in the hope that he might set them both free from the bondage of her frigidity.

And there was still the envy of others to sustain him. He would watch her with other men, delighted by the fascination she held for them, proud of her power to enchant any man who came within range of her influence. None of these men could have her. She belonged to Rheuben. She was his wife, his darling, his possession, and she would take his arm or touch his hand so that everyone would know exactly where she belonged.

So if Rheuben was unhappy and frustrated, he also found a great deal in the marriage to be grateful for. His wife was stunning. He adored her. She did all she could to make his life comfortable. She clung to him and seemed to need the protective circle of his arms. His career was bounding forward. He earned a great deal of money and a promising future lay before him. It was at this stage that Rheuben decided that it was time for Judith to have a child.

JUDITH

Judith continued to float on the surface of life, moving up and down on the ocean swells but never, never allowing herself to be submerged. Rheuben was quite wrong in thinking that her nature was enigmatic. It was not. She was not hiding her inner self from him. The thing she was hiding was her own shallowness. When he tried to discuss their relationship or asked her what she thought of some vital life issue, she was not refusing to reveal her thoughts to him; she was simply unable to reveal them to herself. Survival depended upon maintaining sanity and Judith sensed, in a very sure if inexplicable way, that her sanity depended upon never diving beneath the surface. If ever the waves proved too strong, if ever she should find herself in the depths, she felt that she would face an underworld of such shattering and distorted visions that she would never be able to swim to the surface again. She would, assuredly, drown.

So she spent her days in activity; in work, housework, gardening, cooking, reading. She liked to do such things because they filled up all the spaces and there was not time to feel the emptiness that might otherwise pervade her. Her life with Rheuben was full to overflowing and if he felt some unhappiness and some dissatisfaction, she certainly did not. She was nourished and made secure by his love.

When Rheuben suggested that it was time for her to have a child she felt a slight hesitation. She put her reluctance down to a momentary fear of changing what had been six years of orderly, patterned existence. But she soon acquiesced because, after all, two children were part of the life they had planned. She was now twenty-five years old. Certainly, Rheuben was right. It was time to have a child.

She was sure that she would conceive quickly so she decided to give up work and prepare for motherhood. She went to the library and got out books on the development of the foetus, natural childbirth and good parenting.

At first she thought it pleasant to be at home but she had become accustomed to doing the housework and the cooking quickly and efficiently and she found it disturbing to have all day to do what she had previously accomplished in a few hours. She did not know what to do with her time. The morning passed quickly enough but, by mid-afternoon, there was nothing left to do. She would read for a while but then she would become bored and she would wander restlessly about the house looking for something to do until agitation drove her outside and she would walk along the streets of St. Ives or tramp through the bushland for an hour or so to fill in the time. She told herself that this was a normal reaction. She was not used to leisure. It would take her a short while to adjust herself to the change. Soon she would be pregnant. Before she knew it she would be a mother and then, if the books about babies were right, she would have no time to call her own.

Saturdays, especially, were hard to bear. When she had been working full-time, she had been grateful for the fact that Rheuben worked a six-day week. She had used Saturdays to change the beds, wash the sheets and towels and do the once-a-week housework. But now that she was at home, she spread these tasks over Monday to Friday and that left her nothing to do at all on Saturdays. She wished Rheuben would stay home with her but she could not ask it of him. She knew he had to work long hours. He had made his ambition clear. He intended to be a judge by the time he was forty-five. Nothing less would satisfy him.

She knew that other women had friends. On her afternoon walks she had seen them sitting in each other's kitchens, sipping tea and talking, watching their children playing together in the yard. She had seen women at the University drinking coffee together, or sitting in the quadrangle absorbed in talk. She envied them and regretted that such friendships had never been hers. She thought it had something to do with her beauty. She attracted men but she frightened women away. Perhaps it would be different when she had a child. Perhaps other women would no longer find her threatening. Perhaps she would be able to join them in their kitchens or backyards.

Of course, Judith was wrong. She had never had friends because she did not know that the prerequisite to friendship is the ability to confide. If she could not confide in Rheuben, then how could she have confided in anyone else? She had not even learned how to confide in herself.

Saturdays, then, caused Judith a considerable amount of anxiety. There was a Saturday afternoon, about six weeks after Judith had given up work, when heatwave conditions prevailed. It was too hot for any kind of activity and she felt her restlessness mount. She took off her clothes and plunged into her third cold shower of the day, seeking relief from both the heat and her own agitation. She rubbed herself dry with a towel and went into the bedroom. She put on the large fan and let it play on the bed. She sat down naked in front of the mirror to brush her hair. As she brushed, she allowed herself to gaze at her reflection in the mirror.

The more she gazed the more absorbed she became until she felt totally locked into the image in the mirror. The mirror eyes flared, the mirror lips parted and smiled, the mirror hand rose gently to touch the mirrored breast. Slowly the mirror finger tips circled the mirrored nipple. The mirror hand dropped. The mirror pulsed, the mirrored mouth gasped, the mirrored self rose and took Judith to the bed.

She lay on the silken coverlet and allowed the cool air to fan her body. Her hands were slow and gentle and knowing. They set their own pace and time. They ran across her belly, caressed the curve of her hips, spread down her thighs. A thickness in her throat made her breath light and she hardly knew where to begin her exploration of herself. Her breasts longed for attention and she teased them with the soft, fluttery touch of her finger tips. On and on, quicker and quicker, until the teasing made them taut and tight and the nipples rose in torment to be grasped, held, squeezed, hurt. Firmer, harsher grasps at her breasts fired an invisible cord that flared from nipple to cunt. Her hands let go and she grabbed her mound in both hands, fingers firmly pressed to relieve her mountainous desire. She pressed her legs together, squeezing her hands between her thighs until the fingers hurt. Then she let go and spread her legs wide letting her fingers explore her clitoris, her labia, her vagina. Desire became intolerable. She raised her buttocks from the bed and crashed them down in relentless rhythm as she let her hands fly with new-found strength from clitoris to cunt almost plunging her fist into herself and screaming out loud at the moment of shattering climax.

After a while she got up and sat again in front of the mirror. The beauty that had absorbed her now radiated from the mirror and she laughed in sheer exhilaration. As she studied her mirrored self, she saw exactly why men desired her. She understood at last the strength of Rheuben's love. What she felt, as she looked at her image, was a self-love of such frightening intensity that it was matched only by the love she had seen gleaming from Rheuben's eyes.

She hoped that she might share her newfound ability to love. She hoped her body would react to Rheuben's touch as it had responded to her own. But nothing changed. She was as cold as she had always been, unmoved and uninvolved. She urged herself, willed her body to join and become one with his, but without success.

Now she was glad to be left alone. Day after day she found herself drawn to the mirror and the bed to examine, to explore, to indulge in ecstasy. Fortunately she soon conceived, so her newly acquired radiance could easily be explained as the bloom and joy of pregnancy.

The baby that dwelt inside her became the most precious part of herself. She nurtured it and cared for it as if it were the symbol and the source of all that she had found to be good in herself. She had none of the normal mother fears that her baby would be deformed, or ugly, or spastic, or dead. It would be perfect; it would be beautiful and it would be female. Nothing else was possible. She had created within herself a perfect replica of herself.

She spent her days watching herself grow. She massaged her skin three times a day with baby oil to prevent the formation of stretch marks. She rubbed cream into her nipples to keep them soft so that they would not crack and stop the baby feeding after it was born. She massaged her breasts with downward strokes in the shower each day and pressed the outer edges of the aureola together to prepare the ducts for the milk they would need to carry to her child. She brought herself to orgasm gently and carefully for fear of harming the baby in her womb.

She knitted tiny booties, jackets and bonnets in pink and white; cut out and sewed flowery, vyella nightgowns; embroidered and smocked little dresses. She bought a rocking cradle and made pink and white sheets and pillowslips of the finest lawn. She redecorated the baby's room to make it soft and feminine.

Her absorption frightened Rheuben who, only once, dared to say that the baby might be a boy. She gave him a look of such disdain that he thought it better to keep his fears to himself.

As Judith grew larger the baby took on a true identity. Her name was to be Kate and Judith talked to her as if she had already been born. She knew exactly what Kate would look like and exactly how Kate would behave. In her imagination, Judith rehearsed giving birth to her baby, holding her perfect, new-born, naked beauty, putting her to the breast, bathing her, changing her, settling her down to sleep. She knew that her baby would look just like herself and she pictured the way she would dress the child to the best advantage. Most of all she liked to imagine what close friends she and her daughter would be, laughing together and whispering the hours away.

Labour started a week early but she was not afraid. A moment of shock occurred when she found the blood-stain but she had attended natural childbirth classes and knew how to behave. She waited and soon the contractions started. Mild at first, nothing to worry about. She counted and timed the contractions and, when she considered the time to be right, she rang Rheuben at work and told him to come home and drive her to the hospital. Labour lasted ten hours but was perfectly manageable. She did all the proper breathing at the correct times. She kept absolute control over herself and over the birth.

The only thing that Judith could not control was the fact that she gave birth to a red-faced, ugly, squawking, screaming male child.

THE CHILD

'Post-partum depression. Perfectly normal. She'll get over it in no time.' Rheuben was not so sure, despite the constant reassurances he was given by doctors, sisters, nurses. The baby was three days old and Judith was behaving like a robot.

'Stunned, that's all. Shocked. Often happens to women, especially after their first baby. Can't really believe they've become mothers.'

He went to the baby-showing window. The nurses knew him by now. The Sister-in-charge wheeled the baby over, unwrapped him and held him up for Rheuben to look at. Hymie's face in miniature. Ridiculous. An ironic smile touched the corners of Rheuben's mouth. He sighed heavily and turned away. He had brought his parents to see the child. They had wept with joy at the sight of the baby, with its Jewish nose and thick, pouting lips. They longed to love this symbol of their immortality but Rheuben denied them their Jewish grandparent role. He told them that he would not allow the child to undergo anything as barbarous as a ritual circumcision. Their joy had turned to despair and they had carried on as if they were attending a funeral instead of a birth. Appalled by their behaviour, he had quickly led them away.

He went into Judith's room and sat in a chair by the window. It was a private room and it was full of flowers that had been sent by Rheuben's acquaintances and friends. He had asked people not to visit her, saying that she was not well. He sat with her most of the time but he had given up trying to talk with her because she did not seem to be aware of his presence. She lay quietly in the bed, propped up on pillows, staring at the wall. She frightened him. He had tried, the first day, to reassure her, to tell her that he loved her, to tell her that it did not matter, that the next baby would be a girl, that this baby was healthy and strong, that he was delighted to have a son. He knew that she had not heard him.

On the second day they had brought her the baby several times but each time she had shaken her head and said that the baby was not hers. Rheuben felt a surge of panic whenever she denied the baby but the nurses took it so calmly that he was forced to keep his terror to himself. And perhaps they were right to be calm. Today she had not denied the baby. She had held it. She had looked at it. She had put it to her breast and, miracle of miracles, the milk had flowed. The baby had gulped it down, gone red in the face, choked, screamed. Judith had not known what to do but the nurse showed her how to hold the baby and how to lean back a little so that the milk would come out more slowly; how to turn the baby on its stomach or hold it upright on her shoulder to make it burp. The baby had taken more milk and then fallen asleep. Rheuben could feel his own tension relax as the baby calmed down and he could see that the nurse was pleased with Judith. Perhaps everything would be alright after all.

After the nurse had taken the baby away, Rheuben sat on Judith's bed and held her hand. He lay his head on her breast, tucking himself into her neck. How he longed for her to raise her hand, to lift just her fingers and touch his hair and hold his head against her. She did not move. Rheuben got up and went back to the armchair by the window.

Judith hardly felt or saw him. Her controlled and ordered existence had been made chaotic and she was trying to come to terms with the ensuing confusion. Her mind kept spinning through the labour and the birth, repeating and re-enacting every instant of its progress. Her brain reeled in and out of the dizzying birth, pivoting, circling, weaving, culminating always in the climactic expulsion of the baby from her womb. But then the memory would stop. She would be compelled to go back to the beginning of the labour, to start going through it all again, because the real ending to the birth was unacceptable. She could not explain such a thing to Rheuben. She could not even explain it to herself. Her inner walls had been struck down and she was struggling very hard to reconstruct them. It was a formidable task. It required all her attention.

By the time the baby was a week old, Judith appeared to be functioning satisfactorily. It is true that she was cool and distant, spoke very little, did not smile or give any other indication of joy, but she seemed to accept the baby as hers and dealt with it in a detached but efficient manner. The doctor assured Rheuben that such post-natal depressions seldom lasted longer than six weeks. He should be patient with his wife, helpful and understanding. The nurses made jokes as they left, expressing the hope that the baby would allow Rheuben and Judith to get at least a small amount of sleep. He had a fine pair of lungs and had kept the other babies in the nursery awake all night. Smiles. Good luck! Goodbye!

When they arrived home the baby started to cry. That was normal. It was feed time. Judith fed the baby but when the feed was over she felt afraid. In the hospital, at such times, a nurse would come and take the baby away. Judith took the baby to its room and changed its nappy rather clumsily. As soon as Judith put it down in its cradle it began to cry. She rocked the baby back and forth but it kept on crying. She thought she might have put its nappy on badly so she picked the baby up and made sure the nappy pins were closed. The baby went on crying. She thought it might have wind so she tried to burp it, holding it over her shoulder and rubbing its back. The baby kept on crying. She thought it mightn't have had enough milk so she offered it the breast. It refused and went on crying. She put it back in its cradle and tried rocking it again. Nothing she did had any effect on the baby's crying.

It was a very angry baby. It screamed and shook its fists and kicked its legs. It screamed to be fed; it screamed after it was fed; it screamed before its nappy was changed; it screamed after its nappy was changed; it screamed in the bath and it screamed in the pram. Not only did it scream, it also pissed and vomited and covered itself with shit. All these things seemed intolerable to Rheuben and Judith. He had wanted a nice, happy, smiling son; something he could be proud of. She had wanted a beautiful and perfectly well-behaved daughter, the image of herself.

Rheuben escaped to work and did so as early as possible each morning. He came home at night with the greatest reluctance. This was not what he had envisaged at all. The baby disturbed the pattern of his life. It screamed in the middle of the night and interrupted his sleep. Sometimes Judith did not wake up and he would have to get up himself and pick up the baby. He would change it and try to soothe it but it would never stop crying for him and he would find himself shaking, shaking, shaking it until its eyes rolled and its head wobbled on its neck. When he shook it, it would stop crying for a while but as soon as he got back into bed it would start wailing again. He would plug his ears with cotton-wool to block out its cries but the screams still managed to get through and they filled his skull, echoing and reverberating, despite all his efforts to shut them out. It had to stop but Rheuben did not know how to make it stop.

Judith did not know how to make it stop either. She hated to be left alone with the baby during the day. She would feed it and put it down, hoping that it would sleep but it never would. She would try to pretend that it was not crying but sooner or later its cries pierced through to her. Sometimes she would hold her hands over her ears and scream herself, louder and louder and louder until her own howling drowned out the sounds of the baby.

After three weeks, Rheuben decided that something had to be done. Judith's depression had not lifted. She performed her tasks as a wife and mother with frightening detachment. He was angry and bitter all the time even carrying this mood with him to work. He wanted to blame Judith for the child's crying and could hardly stop himself lashing out at her. He went to the local doctor and persuaded him to prescribe something to make the baby sleep. The doctor insisted, however, that the baby should be given the sedative only at night.

Rheuben found life tolerable again. He could sleep. He could enjoy his work again. Except for Sundays, he could almost put aside the problems of early fatherhood. The baby was four weeks old. He thought he would just be able to survive the next two weeks, by which time, so he had been assured, Judith might be expected to return to normal.

He was, however, expecting the impossible. Judith flirted with normality; she saw brief and flashing glimpses of it, but she was quite unable to take hold of it.

The baby terrified her. When it grasped at her breast and clamped its gums on her nipple, her womb contracted with horror. When it pummelled and punched, when it yelled and roared, its anger entered her and fused with her and she could feel its rage pounding through her veins and hammering in her heart. She could not separate herself from its fury and she did not know what to do with the explosive force that the baby evoked in her.

Instinct, primal and raw, banned for a lifetime, was now unleashed in Judith. She did not know how it would end. She did not know where to turn.

One afternoon, when she could not bear to listen to the baby's cries any longer, she left it in the house and walked to the Baby Health Clinic in St. Ives. She sat in the waiting room with the other mothers. She watched them holding their babies on their knees, soothing, playing, smiling, coaxing. Watching them made Judith feel quite calm and she did not notice that they all looked at her strangely, wondering what she was doing there without a baby.

When it was her turn, Judith went inside. The sister smiled at her. Judith sat down. She began to tell the Sister that she had a baby at home but then the words stopped. The Sister was kind. She spoke quietly to Judith, asking her questions. When was the baby born? Was it a boy or a girl? How much did it weigh at birth? How much did it weigh now? How often was it fed? Was it breast fed or bottle fed? Did she have any problems with the baby? Why hadn't she brought the baby with her?

Judith wanted to speak. She knew that the questions she was being asked were reasonable. She knew that questions such as these must have answers but she could not work out what the answers should be. She wanted to be able to reply but there were no answers in her head and so she could not get any words to come out of her mouth. She began to feel that she should not have come to the clinic so she got up quickly and walked out.

The next afternoon, Judith was determined to be calm. She fed the baby at two o'clock and then took it for a walk in the pram. It behaved quite well and seemed to enjoy looking at the sky and the trees. Then she brought it home and put it to bed. It was quiet for a few moments and Judith went into the lounge-room and sat down. Then it began to whimper, intermittently, half-heartedly. Judith ignored it. She knew there was nothing wrong with the baby. It had been fed, changed, taken on an outing. She had done all that could be expected of her. She was going to read a book and forget that the baby existed. The whimper became a cry, the cry became a scream, the scream became a shriek, the shrieking gave way to a relentless wail that permeated every corner of the house.

The baby's fury penetrated her, flowed into her, filled her, engulfed her, absorbed her until it was no longer possible to separate herself from its mad and mountainous rage. She flung herself down on the lounge-room floor and put her hands over her ears, moaning and weeping and rocking herself back and forth. She forced herself to crawl up onto the lounge, clawing at the upholstery. She made herself look up and out into the back garden and what she saw, with swift, shocking clarity, was the vision of her mother and her baby brother consumed in soaring flames. She could hear her father's cries and joined him in a howl that started in her bowels, gathered force as it roared through her belly, hurling itself free through her clogged and choking throat.

She rushed out of the house and slammed the door. She ran down the street and she did not stop until she arrived, breathless, at the Baby Health Clinic. She ignored the women in the waiting room and, dishevelled and distraught, burst into the Sister's office.

The clinic Sister was angry. She looked at Judith with distaste and told her that she was behaving very rudely indeed. Couldn't she see that the Sister was busy with a mother and baby and that she had a waiting room full of mothers and babies? If Judith wanted any help with her baby she should go home, right this minute, and get the baby. Then she could come back to the clinic and wait her turn.

Judith rushed out of the office, through the waiting room and ran all the way home, her chest aching, her throat emitting harsh, guttural sobs, nose running, tears spilling out of her eyes. She let herself into the house and locked the door. She did not know what would happen.

A sharp fury shot from head to heart to hand and she did not know how to quell it. She went upstairs to the baby's room and opened the door but she was met by silence. The baby had somehow managed to scream itself to sleep.

The next morning the baby woke up at six o'clock. Judith got up and fed it and then put it back to bed. Following its usual pattern, it began to cry. She refused to listen. She had a shower and washed her hair. She went into the kitchen and made herself breakfast. She turned the radio up loud to drown out the baby's cries. She washed up and made the bed. She went to the laundry and put on a wash of nappies. She got out the vacuum cleaner and vacuumed the downstairs carpets. By now it was half-past nine.

She went to the baby's room and got the baby's bath. She took it into the bathroom and half filled it with luke-warm water. She brought it back into the bedroom and put it on its stand. She picked up the baby. He was exhausted from crying and his face was hot and red and crumpled. He smelled of urine and stale milk. She stripped off his clothes and threw them on the floor. She put his wet nappy in a bucket under the change-table. She put one hand under his neck to support his head and the other under his bottom and carried him, still crying, over to his bath. As she slid him into the warm water his crying stopped. Her left hand held his shoulder and his head was supported on her left arm. Her right hand was free to wash him. He kicked his legs. He seemed to be enjoying himself. But soon he began to cry again. She felt quite calm. She was not going to allow him to disturb her.

The bay's screams became angrier, louder, shriller. He threw out his arms and legs; he wriggled and squirmed and twisted himself in Judith's soapy hands. The baby was so furious that he jerked himself free of her slippery hold and slid, with bump, under the water. Judith knew that she had to pull the baby out of the water but she couldn't make herself move. She watched, fascinated. The baby looked startled, coughed, spluttered. She saw his clenched fist open, watched his mouth fill with water. The legs involuntarily kicked; the arms momentarily flayed; the eyes stayed wide open. The scream was subdued to a gurgle. Judith watched the baby for a long time. She watched him until he was quite silent and quite still. She watched him as he rose to the surface and floated there, motionless.

Then Judith wiped her hands on a towel, walked out of the baby's room and went into the bedroom. Her clothes had been splashed with water so she took them off. She sat down in front of the mirror. Her hair was almost dry. She brushed it lovingly, with long, luxuriant strokes. She looked at herself in the mirror and breathed in the deep silence of the house. She had the whole day to herself. She smiled at her mirrored image. In the mirror she could see, behind her, the reflection of the bed. She smiled again, anticipating the cool welcoming touch of the silken coverlet.

Also available from Leone Sperling

COINS FOR THE FERRYMAN

ONE

She has come to visit me. Bundling, grey efficiency – severe-faced, square-jawed, high cheek-boned, rouged, slim-waisted, small-breasted, neatly packaged in round-necked, pastel-coloured, candy-striped dress – my mother.

It is Friday, 10am. Her eyes dart guarded glances at my untidy lounge room. The deep, soft, gold and maroon tapestry-patterned bean-bag chairs flop in comfortable disarray. I can almost discern, in their disordered curves, the imprint of the four little bodies that, last night, nested curled in their velvet warmth.

She looks around. Her hands itch. She picks up a doll with a vegemite face. She cannot hide her distaste. She longs to scream at me, wants to shout out her disgust, ask me how I can possibly live in such a filthy, unhygienic mess. She says nothing. She keeps herself in control. I want her to shout at me so that I can shout back at her. I want her to attack me so that I can defend myself. But in my family no one shouts. We keep our screams locked carefully below throat level. Our howls reverberate in our bellies. We never, never let them out.

'Would you like a cup of coffee?' I ask politely, showing that I know how to play the game, not allowing the aggressive 'What are you doing here? What do you want?' questions to rise any further than my navel.

She can't help it. While I'm putting on the kettle she has to gather the dirty breakfast dishes, scrape the greasy bits of bacon and half-eaten toast off the plates.

'I'll just wash up these few dishes, dear,' she says, 'while you're making the coffee.'

I want to tell her not to wash them up, but the words don't come out. I feel an angry scream mounting inside me but I squash it down and make a grab for a leftover piece of cold toast before it disappears into the rubbish bin. I half chew it and swallow it down quickly to keep the scream from surfacing.

'I thought I would come and give you a hand,' she says.

'I don't need any help,' I reply. Have I actually said the words? I'm not sure. Maybe they are just the words that I would like to be able to say. She goes on as if I haven't said them so I assume I've kept quiet.

'I thought,' she continues, 'that as you're going away on Sunday, you might need some help to get things cleaned up before you leave.'

'I don't need any help.' This time I'm damned sure I've said the words out loud, but she still goes on as if I haven't. I take the biggest apple I can see in the fruit bowl and tear off an enormous bite with my teeth. I keep chewing while she talks to me.

'You don't have it easy,' she says, you girls today. Not like my day. I always had a maid to help me. Look at you – divorced, alone with four children, a big house to run, a full-time teaching job. It's not easy, not easy at all.

I swallow my mouthful of apple and take a deep breath. I speak very loudly and very clearly. 'I don't need any help.' She looks hurt.

'Thanks very much for offering, Mum, but I can do it myself.' A year ago I couldn't have said it. A year ago I'd have let her bulldoze her way through our belongings and create order out of our chaos.

She sits down to drink her coffee. 'Well, dear,' she says, 'I'll just have a cup of coffee with you before I go.' I have defied her, but now some inner force compels me to open the biscuit cupboard. My hands take out the new packet of chocolate biscuits. My fingers tear off the cellophane wrapping and then from hand to mouth the biscuits go – shove, crunch, swallow.

She pretends not to notice what I'm doing in the hope of hiding her horror. She thinks that if she ignores what I'm doing then I'll stop doing it. She's wrong. I would like to be able to stop eating the chocolate biscuits but I don't know how to do that. She keeps on pretending that she's not watching me. But I know she's watching me and that makes it impossible for me to stop. She would like to grab hold of me and shake me and make me stop. She would like to scream, 'How can you be such a pig!' But she sticks to the rules, confining her scream to her eyes.

I think I'm going to vomit. I wish I would. But I know I won't. I never vomit. My stomach's made of elastic.

'You really need to get away, dear, don't you,' she says, sympathetically.

'Yes, I do,' I reply, struggling for control.

'You know, dear,' she goes on, trying not to count the exact number of biscuits I've eaten, 'when you get to London you must book yourself up on organized tours. Believe me, it's the only way to travel. That's what Daddy and I have found. Someone else does all the worrying for you. And you meet such nice people. People who speak your own language. I mean otherwise, dear, you might be very lonely, mightn't you, going overseas for six weeks all by yourself.'

I stare at her, through her. She goes on talking. I retreat. I don't know what she's talking about. Going overseas 'alone'. What does she mean? Doesn't she see that, on my life's journey, I am constantly accompanied by two grandmothers, three aunts, five cousins, one brother, one sister, one father, an ex-husband and four children? Above all, doesn't she realize that I always carry her iron-grey image around with me? Doesn't she understand that I'll be taking her overseas with me? Hopefully I'll lose her – somewhere along the way.

She leaves and I am alone with myself and my thoughts, my house and my mess to puddle and muddle and sift through and order. And I do it, in my own quiet, chaotic way. By the end of the day I have achieved a semblance of order that my children would regard as tolerable. If the dining room table is still piled high with the favourite possessions of four small people, then who cares? We never eat at the dining room table anyway. To the five of us, our mess connotes warmth, love, friendliness. Why should we care if it offends the eye of the outsider? We are snug and warm and secure in our sea of dolls and cars and guns and books and sticky, soft caresses.

My eyes fill with tears. I allow the trickling warmth to tumble down my cheeks. Can I bear to leave them, to be separate from them, for six whole weeks? How will they manage without me? I'm forty years old. Time, surely, to go off on my own for a while – to have a look at the world, to have a look at myself. Of course they can manage without me.

Time, too, I realize, to pick them up from school. It is the last dreary day before the long summer holidays begin. My three sons come bounding out of the gate. How little it takes to make their eyes shine – a hailstorm, a rainbow, an ice cream, the last day of school. I try to look at them objectively and can't. Surely anyone would find them beautiful. The oldest boy – large, placid, responsible, almond-eyed. The second – little, nuggety, tough, aggressive, black cherry eyes. The third – precious, gentle, sensitive, blonde-curled, soft-lipped. They all want to talk at once. It's impossible. I shout for silence, allot turns (youngest first) and each boy's news bubbles out. They are all high on holidays.

We pick up the littlest one. She is waiting anxiously. Tiny, exotic, dark-haired, delicate girl-child. I pick her up and hug her and feel her little arms about my neck. She tolerates my show of affection because she hasn't seen me all day. We bundle into the car and they talk excitedly of holidays and fun, of beaches and picnics, of films they want to see, of Christmas Day at Grandma's house, of presents they might get. Suddenly someone mentions the fact that I will not be there. An appalling silence descends upon us all.

* * * * *

'I understand,' she says, with absolute assurance, 'that you need to be on your own for a while. When I grow up, she goes on, 'I'll want to be alone for a while too.'

It is Sunday. 10am. The day I am due to leave on the grand world tour. She is sitting up on the bench next to me, while I wash up the breakfast dishes. She is six years old.

I don't know what to say to her.

'Will it upset you,' I ask, 'to stay with Grandma and with Daddy while I'm away?'

'Not at all,' she replies. She goes on, 'It's perfectly natural for you to want to be alone. You might,' she adds, 'even write some more stories while you're away.' I want to dry my hands, hug her, kiss her, tell her I love her, tell her it's not her I want to leave, tell her she must know how much I love her, explain to her that its just that I need to be alone for a while, need to sort myself out, see where I'm going. But she's not asking me for reassurance, she's not begging for love, so I can't give it to her.

I go on washing-up and I listen to the chatter.

Why is she so secure and why am I so insecure? My mother's words on the telephone half an hour ago still echo in my ears – 'Not coming to the airport … such a hot day …you don't mind, do you dear? …such big crowds … not coming to say goodbye.' I am shocked numb. I cannot believe she will not come.

I finish in the kitchen and go into my bedroom to pack my suitcase. I know exactly what I'm taking so it's not a difficult task to carry out. While I'm packing my mind goes back to yesterday.

It is Saturday. 1pm. It's my last full day with the children and I want them to be happy. 'Take us to Luna Park!' they all beg and plead. I hate Luna Park. I always refuse to take them there. I must be feeling terribly guilty about going away without them because I find myself agreeing to take them. They are unbelievably ecstatic.

As soon as we get there, they make me go on some dreadful machine that twirls me into space. I am quite sure I'm going to die. I can't even open up my eyes. They laugh at my terror. They get more pleasure from my fear than they do from the monstrous contraption we're riding on. I realize how afraid I am to leave the face of Mother Earth. Yet my children can leave it with defiant laughter, positive that no harm will come to them.

They make me go on the Ferris wheel. I'm not too bad while it's moving, but it keeps stopping to let more people on. Every time it stops I feel an overwhelming urge to jump off and smash myself on the ground below. I cling on to the two littlest children as if their tiny hands can hold my compulsion down.

They look at my terror. They shriek delightedly to each other, 'Look at Mummy! She's so scared she has to hold on to us. Look at her! Look at her!'

'Don't move!' I yell at them. 'Don't move! You'll fall!' They are doubled up with laughter. The more they laugh the more they move. The more they move the more terrified I become. I see all five of us – a mound of indecipherable arms and legs, blood, flesh, brains emptying onto the pavement.

Thank God! It's not going to stop any more – it's going to keep moving. We just might survive after all. I find it's alright when the wheel is coming downwards towards the ground but when I am drawn upwards, away from the earth, my entire being shrieks a silent protest. The ride ends. They have to help me off. I am totally disordered. They sit me down. Their laughter turns to concern. They fuss over me. 'Are you alright, Mum?' 'Do you feel sick?' 'Can I get you a drink?' I am so shattered I cannot even reply. This is ridiculous. I don't want to frighten them. This is their day. We are all supposed to be having fun. With enormous effort I pull myself back to them. I laugh at myself. 'What a stupid mother I am, to be so afraid of heights.'

They are reassured. They like me to see myself in the role of 'stupid mother'. It makes them feel more grown up. I send them off with a few dollars to buy themselves ice creams while I get on quietly with the process of knitting myself together again. By the time they get back I'm all in one piece.

I've been 'good' so far today. Being 'good' means eating healthy foods, like meat and eggs and fruit and vegetables. Being 'good' means eating no bread and no cakes and no sweets and no chocolate biscuits. I've found, to my great surprise, that there's a health food shop at Luna Park. You can actually buy yoghurt instead of hot-dogs and fairy-floss. I'm pleased with myself for having been 'good' today.

My daughter suddenly hands me a sticky, dripping ice cream. 'I've had enough,' she says. Its melting sweetness is inside my mouth before I realize what's happened. One mouthful is all it needs for me to lose the battle for the day. For the rest of the afternoon I join the children on an endless orgy or waffles, ice cream, hot chips, soft drinks, lollies and fairy-floss until we all stagger to the car. They are full, warmly satisfied. A great day. I am bloated with despair. If I cannot cope with a Ferris wheel, how the hell am I going to cope with a jumbo jet?

I come back to my bedroom and my packing and to the two biggest boys bursting into my room, asking me how much money I'll give them to spend at the airport.

They are so calm. They behave as if today were any ordinary day. I feed on their tranquility and realize that they are quite able to let me go. They know I'll come back. They know that our circle of loving will always be there – warm, complete, secure.

How I wish I could be like them, but my mother's words are still banging away there inside my head – 'Not coming to the airport' – and I am forced to face the extraordinary truth that not one of my children is bound to me as I am bound to her.

They help me put my things in the car and we go off for our final treat. We are going to a Chinese restaurant for lunch and afterwards to the airport. My plane is due to leave at 4pm.

They love Chinese food and I don't mind taking them because it's always possible to be 'good' at a Chinese restaurant. I'm happy to stick to meat and vegetable dishes. Not like McDonald's. That's a nightmare. At McDonald's I am constantly faced with the temptation of Big Macs and French fries and ice cream sundaes with hot caramel sauce. At a Chinese restaurant I feel reasonably safe.

I'm very on edge. Anxiety. Terror. Anticipation. I remind myself, between the vegetable soup and the beef chop suey, that I've never been on my own for any sustained period of time. I have gone from belonging to belonging; from school to university to marriage; from parental home to marital home; from being a child to being a wife to being a mother. There has never been a time when I have been responsible only to myself, belonged only to myself.

I feel that I ought to reprimand my third son, who is eight years old, for shoveling beef and oyster sauce into his mouth with a spoon and a hand instead of with a spoon and a fork. I stop myself. He is having such a marvelous time, gravy all over his hands and face. The frequent reprimands of my children's father momentarily disturb me, almost prompt me to tell my son to use his fork. 'Why can't you teach them some table manners! They can't even use a knife and fork properly.' He's right. They do embarrass him when he takes them out. But if I do reprimand my son it will be with his father's voice, not my own. He's not embarrassing me. I don't give a damn. I just enjoy watching his total immersion in messy pleasure. I win over the father's voice. I say nothing to my son. No! Damn it! I haven't won at all because suddenly I'm asking my daughter if she really wants all the rice she's ordered and she gives me some and before I know it I'm shoving rice into my mouth. Now I know for certain that when I buy them an ice-block after the Chinese meal, I'll have to buy one for myself as well. They'll be satisfied with water ice-blocks. I'm going to need an ice cream, probably with chocolate coating. I sink into despair. I am nothing but my mouth. I fuse with the food. I am the food. I cannot distinguish the boundaries of my self. I cease to exist. The avalanching, rumbling monster in my belly asserts himself again.

I try to picture him. He is a lion, roaring there in the dark hollow of my insides, demanding his right to gobble people up. I don't want him to gobble people up and, above all, I don't want anyone to know that he's inside me so I keep throwing him chunks of food to keep him quiet. I know I have to come to terms with him. If he and I are both going to inhabit this body for the rest of its life then we're going to have to understand each other. It seems to me that I'm always considerate about his needs but he doesn't make much effort to understand mine. At times I've thought of trying to exorcise him. But if I got him out of myself what would be left? How would I fill the gaping hole he left behind? Would there be anything left? Or am I synonymous with my lion; are he and I one entity and if I let him die would I die too? I don't know. So I keep on feeding him – just in case.

Am I mad? I don't really know but I don't think so. It all makes sense to me. I am born under the star of Leo and I carry my sign within me. A few times I've tried to tell people about it but when I do so I sense that they think what I'm saying is peculiar so I've learned to keep quiet about it, most of the time.

I don't just buy them ice-blocks. I become generous. I let them buy peppermint creams and thin, round, dark-chocolate discs from the expensive sweet shop that is just over the road from the Chinese restaurant. They can't believe their luck but my generosity is deceptive. I'm being cunning. I know that this shop sells mouth-watering Turkish Delight. My stomach is full but there is no connection between hunger and my need to eat. I have to have the sweet. I buy a whole pound. It's terribly rich. Any normal person would be satisfied with one or two pieces. I eat the lot. In five minutes it's all gone.

I want to vomit. I long to vomit. The rich, sticky sweetness nauseates me. I feel five months pregnant, my stomach distended and sore. I berate myself. 'You disgusting gluttonous pig,' I say to myself. I become the Turkish Delight, quivering, jelly-fat. I hate myself. I long for the day to be over. Tomorrow will be a new day, a new start, a new chance.

I always long for the magic of Mondays, a new beginning of a new week and if the first of the month happens to fall on a Monday then it seems to me that I have a double chance to start anew, to be 'good'. Maybe, just maybe, I will have the strength to get through a whole week, even a whole month, without stuffing myself with food. It never happens, of course. I'm so anxious about it being Monday that I'm usually shoveling food into myself by mid-morning.

I went to a hypnotist once. He stopped me from smoking and I thought he might be able to stop me from eating. It didn't work though. Sometimes, for no apparent reason, it goes away for a while and I actually stay on a diet for months and months. I get really slim and as soon as that happens I start eating again and put on all the weight I've lost. I once told myself that if it hadn't gone away by the time I was forty I'd kill myself. I'm forty now and it hasn't gone away. I can't very well kill myself though, can I? I've got four children relying on me.

And it happened again last night. It hasn't happened for years. I had a dream. People kept coming into my room, lots of people – my brother, my sister, Mum and Dad, men I've known. They held up a big white sheet next to my bed or maybe it was a flag – yes, that's right – an American flag or a Union Jack. I thought they might wrap me up in it. Perhaps it was my shroud. But they didn't. They just held it up so that I couldn't see behind it. I heard noises, though. I knew they were all screwing behind that flag and I was all alone; no one was making love to me and I felt so lonely that I started to cry and suddenly I couldn't breathe – I was choking, choking, choking and I woke up and I was suffocating, my face squashed in the pillow and I had to use every bit of strength I've got to force myself up on to my arms, to get my face out of the pillow that was smothering me, suffocating me, killing me. I was wide awake then, wet, shaking. I'll die that way. One day I'll dream my suffocating dream and it will really happen. I know that's the way I'll go back.

I've dreamed similar dreams ever since I can remember. At one time it frightened me so much that I wouldn't go to sleep. I was eighteen years old. I was sure I was going to die if I let myself go to sleep. She had to sit on my bed and keep me calm until I fell asleep. Like a mother should - for her baby.

She thinks I've forgotten but I haven't. I remember being born. No one believes me when I say that so it's another thing I've learned to keep quiet about. But I do remember. I remember before I was born too. I remember swimming soft in the sunlight of the womb, rocked gentle, lulled, swaying in her belly. I remember that I preferred to breathe through our chord, our harmony of food and air, complete and total flow. I never wanted to be born at all. She and I – so separate, so remote, so far from understanding each other; she and I were one once, tuned in to each other's needs. I moved when she moved, stopped when she stopped, started with fright at her fears, cried when she cried, laughed when she laughed. Fused together.

No wonder I resisted her efforts to expel me. I could not understand why I shouldn't stay in there forever. She'd been quite happy about our union for nine months, why did she now jerk and move the walls of my fortress, make them hard and rigid, drain away my soft fluid bed? Dry and harsh she became, forcing me movement by movement down her hostile canal, muscles contracting upon me, pushing, pushing, pushing me out into the stabbing air, the bright-lit sterility. And in her haste to rid herself of me she didn't even notice that she'd let the cord wind itself around my neck so that the moment of my birth was fired with harsh, rasping, choking strangulation. Life and death mingled at my cold awakening on that bleak August day.

When I was a child I often dreamed of being chased and strangled by a long pink snake lady. It was not so much the chase that frightened me, not even the strangulation. What frightened me was the end of the dream, the moment when I realized that the face of the snake lady was exactly the same as the face of my mother.

* * * * *

I am at the airport. Sunday 3pm. I feel so separate from myself that for a moment I can't understand what on earth I'm doing here. They want money for lollies, drinks, to play the games on the machines. I keep doling it out. I don't care what it costs, as long as they are happy, as long as they don't cry. Please, God, if you exist don't let them cry.

I go to the check-in counter. It's a sweltering day. My clothes are wet. I have to carry a heavy sheepskin coat. Suddenly I remember a dream I had a few nights ago. In my dream I was standing, just as I am now, waiting to check in before boarding the plane. In my dream it was terribly hot, just as it is today. In my dream they called out our flight number and then read out the London weather report – 'Sleet, snow, temperatures below zero, freezing, rain.' I looked down at my clothes and saw that I was wearing a thin cotton dress and realized, at the same moment, that I had left my sheepskin coat at home. 'I've forgotten my coat. I've got to go home and get my coat!' Although I shouted and screamed I was locked in the crowd and they carried me, coatless, onto the plane. I felt the terror of knowing that when I reached London I would inevitably freeze to death.

The shock of the dream shivers through me and despite the heatwave conditions I clutch my sheepskin coat fiercely to me.

I am at the head of the check-in queue. My hand wets the plastic folder that holds my ticket, passport, traveller's cheques.

'Ticket please,' she says. I give her my ticket. I am very neurotic about my passport. I hope she won't ask for it. The reason I'm so neurotic about my passport is that I went through such trauma to acquire it. The red tape involved in digging up certified copies of marriage and divorce papers was bad enough. So was the implied insult from the Officer in the Immigration Department who felt that no adult lady could possibly be only 143 centimetres in height. But, worst of all, was my trip to the Registrar General's Department where my request for a copy of my birth certificate was met with the extraordinary reply that my birth had never been registered.

'It has to be there,' I told them. They checked again. There is a record of my older brother's birth; there is a record of my younger sister's birth. I feel negated. Wiped out. Why did they forget to register my birth? I ask them why. They say to each other:

'I thought you did it, Mummy dear.'

'No, dear, it was always your job to register the births.'

'Where do you want to sit,' she asks, 'aisle or window seat?' I am about to say I don't care when my friend interrupts. He has come to the airport to say goodbye to me and to take my children back to their father's house. He has had a premonition that my plane will crash.

'She'll sit right at the back of the plane,' he interjects, 'in the last row.' He doesn't want me to go. He thinks he loves me. He thinks I'll screw ten different men every day. He thinks I'll forget him. He might be right. So he's invented the idea that my plane will crash. The certain knowledge of my death has come to him in a dream. He's had other dreams like this before. They always come true. Normally such foreboding would terrify me, but this time it doesn't. I tell him again that the plane won't crash and that I refuse to die. I'm not sure that I believe what I'm saying but by now I feel swept along too far to turn back. I've got a real sense of inevitability right now. I just know that I am going to get on that plane and go.

My third little boy flings himself into my arms and has started to give me the 10,174 kisses that he has calculated he will require to see him through the next six weeks. He is the only one I am worried about. He seems to need me so much. I know the others are self-assured enough to cope. We peck at each other, little mouth kisses, lip to lip, endlessly building his fortress of love. I suddenly wonder how he'll manage to shit while I'm away. He has some anxiety about shitting. He never does it at school or at anyone else's place. He always waits for me. 'Start me off,' he says. That means I have to stand at the toilet door while he starts. After the first 'plop' he's safe and tells me I can go away. Can he go for six weeks without a shit? I don't suppose he can. It's better than it used to be. I used to have to sit on the floor outside the toilet and talk to him the whole time.

Sometimes he develops a compulsive sniff, or his eyes twitch, or he looks at the palms of his hands and then at the soles of his feet. The symptoms are always on the move. He never sticks to any of them for too long. And he can't drink any soft drink if anyone else has drunk out of the bottle and he can't eat his dinner if anyone else breathes on it. And, above all, he can't bear to look at straight arms. No one in the family is allowed to hold their arms out straight. I don't know why. But we all understand about his little peculiarities and he has managed to carve out for himself an area of tolerance that is given to no one else in the family. He gets migraines, too, but we all ignore them. He just lies upside down on the big bean-bag chair and falls asleep and he's all better in an hour or two. I've asked the other kids to look after him but will the adults who mind him understand? He lives on some other level of reality. He just visits us occasionally but whenever he comes to call he needs so much reassurance and love before he flits off again to his own, more interesting, realm of existence.

We're up to kiss number 764 when I suddenly hug him to me. Precious, curly-haired, ageless child. 'You'll be alright, won't you?' I ask fiercely.

'Seven-hundred-and-sixty-five, seven-hundred-and-sixty-six,' he goes on, unable to be distracted from his compulsive counting.

Everything to him is a matter of numbers. As soon as he meets someone he wants to know how old they are. He's not being rude. He just needs a new jumping off point for his endless calculations. The patter goes something like this: 'If you're twenty-four years old then you're three times as old as I am and you're fifty-two years younger than Grandpa and sixteen years younger than Mummy. You might think I'll never be half your age but when you're thirty-two, I'll be sixteen and then I'll be half as old as you are.' It doesn't stop there. It goes on and on. At first you feel some need to check his calculations. Then you realize you're not supposed to do that. There's no doubt that he's right. You just have to keep nodding your head and mumbling, 'Yes'. He can't read very well and when he writes he holds his pencil in such a peculiar way that his letters emerge on the page as a spidery code of hieroglyphics. He thinks he isn't clever. I suspect he's a genius. We are up to kiss number 801. I go on and on because that's what he needs and I resist the desire to crush my warmth and my love into his little body.

'That'll do,' he says. 'I don't need as many as I thought I did.' I am relieved. I have visions of myself not being able to board the plane because we have not reached the magical number that will set him free.

My friend stands beside me, bleak. As my flight number is called he hugs me to him and I feel his tears on my cheek. Then I start to cry and I am bewildered. The children do not cry and they do not understand why we do. I have been so worried that they would be the ones to break down and now the sight of this adult crying absolutely undoes me. I break away from him and give my children a final hug. The two smallest ones are silent. I sense their state of shock. 'Have a good time,' the two big ones say, almost in unison, embarrassed by my tears.

I look at her, the littlest. In her tense eyes I see the wish to rush after me. She grabs her biggest brother's hand. He helps her hold herself back. She would like to spring from the crowd of people and dive into the plane with me. My last sight is of her tiny face, lips firmly pressed, holding back. I can't risk turning around. I dare not look at them again.

COINS FOR THE FERRYMAN
is available for Kindle, iBooks and POD at

www.cilentopublishing.com

AUTHOR'S BIOGRAPHY

Leone Sperling was born in Sydney in 1937, attended Sydney Girls' High School and graduated from Sydney University with a BA Honours degree in English literature. She taught English full-time with the NSW Department of TAFE for twenty years, a career that she found rewarding and fulfilling. She regards the fact that she did find time to write as a minor miracle because her marriage ended when her children were very young.

Three books, Coins for the Ferryman, Mother's Day and Oasis were published between 1981 and 1990. She was awarded a Literature Board grant in 1985. She has also had several short stories and articles published in national newspapers and Australian anthologies. These are now collected in The Book of Life.

After taking early retirement she wrote two novels, What About Love? and Jamie. She then undertook a four-year naturopathic Diploma in Nutrition. Leone now enjoys close, mutually rewarding relationships with her four children and six grandchildren and studies Latin with Continuing Education at Sydney University. Severe hearing impairment has resulted in the need for a Cochlear implant. For several years Leone has been on the Management Committee of Better Hearing Australia's Sydney branch and spends a considerable amount of time as a research volunteer with Cochlear and with the National Acoustic Laboratories.

Leone's writing is open and honest. Her style is spare and simple but constantly displays a willingness to confront and examine both the joyful and the darker aspects of human emotions and relationships.

www.ingramcontent.com/pod-product-compliance
Lightning Source LLC
Chambersburg PA
CBHW071523170626
46811CB00007B/2937